INDISCREET

The Agency Dark Affairs Duet
Book One

Amélie S. Duncan

Published by Amélie S. Duncan

Copyright © Amélie S. Duncan, 2018

authorameliesduncan@gmail.com

Cover Design by Sommer Stein and Perfect Pear
Creative

Interior Formatting by Entanglement Publishing

TABLE OF CONTENTS

CHAPTER ONE

W inter had come, as people say on *Game of Thrones* or when they just want to be sassy and empowered about something or someone they got over. I was going for the sassy variety. After seven months of separation and deliberation, my ex-husband, Governor Patrick Walsh Jr., had run out of excuses. He'd finally signed our divorce papers, and the judge had made it final. I was now free to move on, though after six and a half years together, I had no idea how to go about it. That didn't matter right now; the logistics were for worrying about later. Today was all about celebrating starting over.

I was one party down and about to leave for the second one. The first was the annual

Christmas party at Perfetto Cosmetics, the company I ran with Astrid Marin, the executive director and my best friend. We held it on the two floors of our office in downtown Seattle's Westlake building. The celebration included rich catered food, an eye-candy DJ, and prizes, and we made our big announcement—five additional vacation days added on to their holiday week. Our amazing staff danced and sang our praises the rest of the day, and we had more than the holiday to bring us cheer. Our accountant, Dalton Pierce of DP Management, had personally called to let us know we'd had record profit this quarter. Perfetto was on its way to becoming women's first choice in cosmetics.

The second party was more low-key, though not any less noteworthy: my divorce dinner with Astrid at Elation Bistro, the restaurant two doors down from the office. The location was chosen not just out of convenience, but because they had the best, most delicious cocktails in town. I was ready to have a couple, and that was the plan once I finished up with work.

I was about to shut down my computer when Astrid opened my office door. She did it with her usual flourish, jingling a bag of samples from our Summer Heat line, and strutted over to my desk.

"Watch out men, Gia Ruiz is available," she joked.

"Watch out?" I giggled. "More like *come and get me.*"

She laughed with me, but it wasn't just a joke. I had gone without sex for far too long.

I freed the bag from her hand before she, as usual, dumped her belongings on one of the two fabric and steel chairs. Then, pushing aside one of the neat piles of paper and products, she sat down on the edge of the desk.

Until recently, Astrid and I had been the wonder twins around the office. Both of us often wore a variation of black wool designer power suits. Today we had on different shades of button-down shirts; hers was blue while mine was gray. The change came with our hair. While mine was black, wavy, and hung just past my shoulders, she'd chopped hers off to a platinum blonde pixie that made me want to try something different with my own every time I saw it. Speaking of different, I picked up the sample size *Crave Me Crimson* black metallic tube and smeared it across my lips. We had the staff handle most of daily production, but we both enjoyed testing the samples. The marketing notes read: *Perfetto Cosmetics "Crave Me Crimson" lipstick. Target market: 18- to 24-year-olds.*

When I tried on lipstick or any of our cosmetics, I wasn't just assessing how it looked, but more noting the feeling I had when I looked at myself wearing it. What came to mind was what I hadn't felt in years: attractive, captivating, and beautiful. I decided my 28-year-old pucker looked hot as hell in this shade of red. I was killing it, and my confidence didn't go unnoticed by Astrid. Her soft brown eyes squinted. "It's kind of vampy on you with your pale complexion, but sexy."

"I'll take sexy," I mused. Tilting my head upward, I ran my finger over my bottom lip and showed her the lack of transference. "Perfect shine, no smear."

She picked up the sample pack and we tried on the pink, coral, and plum in matte and satin finishes. After using the last of the sample makeup remover wipes, I quickly jotted down on my notepad to schedule a brainstorming session on broadening our target market.

"I like the 'doesn't kiss and tell' part you added to the campaign," she said, providing her feedback.

I beamed. "I do too. I just wonder what I'd wear with such a shocking shade of red." My eyes widened, and so did hers, our light bulbs going off at the same time.

"Sexy Me Stilettos!" we said together.

I swiveled in my black rattan chair and clicked on the computer screen to open the Frisky Frolics app. In a quick search, I found the

Manolo Blahnik red and suede pointed-toe pumps I'd seen that morning and quickly pressed the button to purchase the available pair at Saks.

"We have dinner reservations," she reminded me as she started nosing through my overstuffed handbag for her Christmas gift. Of course, we both knew she enjoyed surprises, and I had already finished shopping before Thanksgiving. It wasn't long before she zeroed in on my e-reader and mused as she scrolled through my library, reading aloud the titles of some of my more obvious erotic choices.

"*Captured, Rescued, and Ravished by the Bad Boy.*" She snickered. "Well, look who's ready to get back into the saddle...or should I say the cuffs?"

My face warmed as I fondly reminisced. *Whew.* That story had set my e-reader on fire. *Loved it.* I snatched the device away and placed it in my handbag. "So what? It's fantasy."

Honestly though, it was more than just a fantasy. Patrick's cheating and my ambition weren't the only problems in our marriage. Mixing it up sexually had been a constant preoccupation of mine for years.

"You know I don't judge at all. I'm the one who recommended you read some of the ones you have on here," she said with a grin. "I'm happy for you. You deserve better. You go for whatever you want, like you told me after my divorce."

I laughed and leaned back in my chair. "Easy for me to say and for you to do. You found your Mr. Perfect." Astrid got that dreamy look on her face, as she should have. She'd found her happily ever after; she was married with a child. For me, I wasn't so sure what my happy ending would be.

"You are witty and clever, you run the hell out of your own business, not to mention that you're beautiful. There are plenty of men who would love to go out with you, even here at the company. In fact, Brent from marketing—"

"No way," I lamented, cutting her off. "I'm not dating anyone I manage."

"You don't have to marry him, just have sex," she teased, waggling her brows.

"Yeah, so I can be water cooler gossip of the week." I smirked. "No thanks."

"Who said you'd get a whole week?" she mused, and we laughed together.

"But seriously," she asked when we calmed down. "How do you feel?"

I bit my lip. "I'm happy about the divorce, but this putting myself out there stuff..."

I didn't finish, and I didn't have to. Astrid got up and gave me a hug. "It'll be hard at first, but look at it this way: you know what you don't want now."

I sighed. I sure did, but tonight wasn't about the woes of the end of my marriage. It was about celebrating. With that in mind, I stuffed the divorce paperwork in my bag and prepared to leave.

Astrid and I put on our winter coats and beige infinity knit scarves, bundling up against the wintery wind. Our leather boots crunched the fresh snow and salt on the sidewalk as we made our way to Elation. We each ordered a steak au poivre and a Christmas-tini. When the drinks were delivered to our table, we raised them up for a toast. "To the next chapter of your life," Astrid said with a smile, and then we clinked our glasses together.

I gulped down half of my drink and motioned for the hostess to get another one. Astrid ordered another too. By the time the food arrived, Astrid had shared every little thing her three-year-old son Jacob had done since I saw him the previous week, when he came to what was supposed to be our relaxing night, along with a long list of holiday parties her husband had to oversee for his corporate management company. Listening to her made it clear that my world had done a one-eighty.

Did I have anything left to share now that I wasn't Patrick's wife?

Realizing I had gone quiet, Astrid reached over and patted my arm. "I just can't believe Patrick," Astrid complained. "He's made the biggest mistake of his life. I mean, with all he has on his plate with his campaign, to cheat on you—"

"Doesn't matter now," I interjected, speaking over her while putting on a smile. "I'm just happy it's over."

"Sorry." She covered her mouth. "I didn't mean to bring it up again. You know we'd love to have you over at our house for Christmas. It bothers me that you'll be alone in that big house."

I shook my head and smiled. I hadn't been in "that big house" but for a few weeks. Between moving and work, I had spent barely any time there, so I had plenty of unpacking to do. "I'll be fine."

"I know, but it could be fun. We'll decorate the tree, and maybe we can discuss some contacts in the area that might help Tim's mayoral bid—"

"I'll give you my contacts for Tim," I replied lightly, but I was certain *that* part of my life was over. I'd help some, but Tim would need to do his own heavy lifting. I tried to remind her I was no longer in politics as gently as I could.

"That would be great," she said. "We're both excited about the possibility of his run, but we're finding it's not easy to navigate. The way you managed Patrick made it look so easy." The tiredness around her eyes made it clear he wasn't the only one who was stressed.

"It's not, and fundraising is only the beginning," I cautioned her again. It was beyond me why she would encourage her husband to get involved in politics after all the stress and pressure she saw in my life—the endless fundraising, soul-crushing ass-kissing, and God-awful obligatory smiling, not to mention all the constant networking. She'd become what I had been: a wife-workhorse. "Thank you for the invitation, but I'll be fine. I'm done with politics. I won't be getting involved in any of it."

She looked at me, puzzled. "I didn't mean it that way, Gia. I invited you because I thought it would be fun, but I understand. Thank you from both of us for the contacts."

I beamed at her and sighed inwardly. She was sick of the campaigning already. "You're very welcome."

"Now for the good stuff," she said, grinning as she pulled out her phone. "I got a list from Tim of all his single friends and acquaintances who we both know would love to meet you."

"Hold that thought," I said. I got up and went to the restroom around the bar. Her husband was nice, but I didn't have the heart to tell her I didn't want a Tim or a Tim-like man. Yes, he was loving, attentive, and a great dad, but he was too much like Patrick—always focused on how to increase his power and profile. I wanted a man who was comfortable and confident in himself, a man who put me first, a man who wanted me.

I washed my hands and fixed my hair before going back to join Astrid.

On my way back to our table, I spotted Liz Crenshaw coming through the entrance. We hadn't seen her in a while so I walked closer to greet her but then stopped—she wasn't alone. She was with an attractive twenty-something man. I was surprised and impressed, not only by his age, but by what he was doing. He grabbed her face and kissed her passionately. His hands moved down to her hips, and then lower. He was touching her in a way I'd never been touched in public before. It was raw, possessive, and passionate. I was enthralled.

Then another man came up to stand next to them. He was the tall, dark, and handsome type, striking in looks and well put together. He was dressed in a leather jacket, designer gray slacks, and a black button-down shirt opened at the collar. He was brooding, but magnificent. He tapped their shoulders and, for a moment, looked my way. I quickly turned my head, finally realizing how rude I'd been by staring. They parted, and I was about to move back to my table when Liz called out to me. "Gia Walsh!"

I turned and took the hug. "It's Ruiz," I reminded her.

"Oh. Congratulations," she said, covering her mouth. Her lips were swollen, and she had a sappy grin on her face. "Sorry, but—"

"No apologies," I cut her off. "Patrick was an asshole."

"Amen," she said.

I laughed. "Astrid's here, want to come over and say hello? You can have dinner or share a dessert with us if you're alone."

She glanced behind her and the men were gone. "Yes, that sounds great. I was going to wait for my friend to finish his meeting at the bar, but it could be a while. We can all catch up." She excused herself for a call and I heard her explain a change in plans to dine with us, then she followed me over to our table where she hugged Astrid. After Liz ordered a potato bisque and salad, Astrid asked her, "What are you planning for the holidays?"

Liz tossed her hair back. "Oh, the usual boring affair."

I arched my brows. She didn't mention her new lover, and for whatever reason, I didn't either, at least not yet. "Same here. I'll probably redecorate or something tedious."

Liz laughed, arching her back in a way that made the V-neck of her tight cashmere sweater dip.

"What is going on with you?" Astrid asked. "You look different."

Liz shrugged and ran her hand through her new long red hair. "I recently got a makeover."

"I'd say it was more than that," I murmured. This went beyond her new highlights and layered hairstyle. She was giving off a sexual charge, and just a glance around the restaurant let me know men were responding by gazing over at Liz. Their looks were curious, their smiles full of admiration. She must have felt them looking, but she didn't discourage them; instead, she just took it in stride.

Yeah, I'll have whatever she's on. I wasn't sure about what had brought this boost in confidence, but I was happy for her, and honestly, downright envious. From the view on the outside, I'd have said she'd hit a gold mine in whatever she was doing now, and I wanted to know more.

"How about another round?" Astrid asked.

"Sure, but I'll be right back," Liz said, rising to go to the restroom. I stood up too, and Astrid minutely shook her head.

"You're going again, Gia?"

I lifted a shoulder. "It's the cocktails." It was a little lie, but I wanted a moment alone with Liz.

She was at the sink putting away her phone when I arrived.

"I saw you sucking face at the door," I said, grinning and poking her shoulder. "Spill."

She laughed gleefully, and I joined in with her. "God, Gia...I mean, when Marco is around, I just forget myself."

I couldn't hide the wide grin that spread across my face. Even his name was sexy. "How did you meet Marco?"

"I may still have the card." She dug in her purse and handed me a black and white card that said *The Agency*. "That's how."

"What is it?" I stared down at it

"It's like a matchmaking service," she said.

I wrinkled my nose. "I hate that shit." I held the card out for her to take back. "No thanks."

She pushed it back toward me. "This one is different. It's exclusive," she explained, leaning against the counter. "What I've found and learned...it's beneficial in many ways."

I shook my head. "Is this another one of those hot new online matchmaking companies? I can't put my photo and information online."

Along with the non-disclosure we'd agreed on to get Patrick to finally sign, he'd added a clause that we both agreed to avoid public relationships until after his re-election the next year, and not to embarrass each other in any scandal. If that happened, it would make the agreement null and I'd have to give him half of the money and property created during our marriage, so I had agreed. It could include some of my family inheritance released during the marriage and dividing up my company, neither of which I would ever risk losing.

"This one is strict about being secretive," she said. "You know how it is with hacking, social media—it's hard to have any privacy. From what I've found, they pride themselves on being discreet. This isn't going online. It's invitation only, but I have no doubt they'll take you. I'll check tonight." She pointed down to the card. "You'll need to present it to gain access to their building."

"So, men like Marco are available at this agency?" I asked.

"Yes, and I would go with you, but we're together now," she boasted brazenly. "I didn't meet him right away. There were other men before him—many."

My mouth dropped open. Well, Liz was full of surprises tonight. "Many? Damn, slow down, woman."

She lowered her head. "I'd only been with Richard. Christmas Eve would have been our tenth anniversary..." Her voice faltered.

I took her hand. Her husband Richard's death the year before had been hard for her. I was happy she was trying to move on with her life. "I was teasing. I'm sorry."

"It's okay. I'm fine," she assured me. "Anyway, his name is Marco and he's wonderful. He treats me like a queen. I would have introduced you to him, but he had a working dinner with his friend Dane Westbrook."

"Dane?" I said in as casual a tone as I could muster. "Was that the name of the other man?"

She blotted her lip and grinned. "Saw him too, eh? You interested? I only just met him. I'm not sure he's available, but The Agency has plenty of good-looking men. They're sure to have whatever you might be looking for. The more detailed you are, the better the match. You can get a man that'll take you for a picnic in the park, or you can go to the other extreme and get one who will tie you up, just like some of those erotica books you were always reading." She giggled.

I powdered my face. "Were? Still am. You have the same books, need I remind you?" I pointed out, laughing. "I'm not interested in being treated like some personal blow-up doll."

She laughed and said, "You don't have to. It's about finding what you want and exploring who you are. I'll make the call for you. Text you later." She moved toward the door.

"Wait, I haven't agreed," I called after her.

She paused in the doorway. "I know how you want to be treated, Gia. Try it out. It's better than being lonely."

"I don't know…" I said. Then again, what did I have to lose? Awkward online dates and mediocre app hook-ups?

Astrid opened the bathroom door then came inside and took our arms. "Come on back to our seats, you two. The food is getting cold at the table."

"We're coming," I said hurriedly, collecting my purse. Before I closed it, I took another glimpse down at the card. It was a chance for a change. I might be able to expand my prospects and find a man more compatible with me; I couldn't just throw that away. I quickly tucked the card into my bag.

CHAPTER TWO

"This is you, Gia," Astrid announced, bringing me out of my head and back to the limo the three of us were sharing for the ride home from the restaurant.

My thoughts were preoccupied for most of the trip, partially due to the buzz from the cocktails. It was also because of Liz's glowing review of her experience with The Agency. Could going to a matchmaking company work the same way for me? I wasn't convinced. It was late, so I quickly said goodbye to them with hugs and promises to get together over the holiday. I exited through the door held open for me at my new home.

Standing on the slate-paved driveway, I stared at the two-story stone and brick craftsman house with a double garage—quite the change from the sprawling governor's mansion in Olympia. In the evening light, I took in its beauty, though the landscape was barely visible under the blanket of snow. The cypress and barberry shrubbery looked picturesque cloaked in white. The best part of it all: the peacefulness.

The second-floor master bedroom was where I headed, and it was the only one I used of the four in the house. I had updated it with a platform bed I'd ordered just before we separated. *That is something I will keep*, I decided after my shower. The demister was on, but still I wiped the steam off the large double mirror to finish up my cleansing routine, and I hesitated at my reflection. The thought of being naked in front of a new man made me nervous. Patrick wasn't one to compliment me, but he always had a word to say when I didn't meet his standards. Now, what would a new man see when I got naked for him?

My face was by far my best feature. Like my mother, I had long, arched brows that didn't require much upkeep, dark brown eyes with long lashes, and full, well-shaped lips. My C-cup breasts were my second-best feature. Sure, I wanted a firmer tummy and buttocks, but doesn't everyone? I'd be all right.

For the six years of our marriage, Patrick had been a rising star in politics. The job came with a team of consultants who imposed a set of restrictions to help him get ahead, and as his partner, I had to follow them too. The number one rule was not to overshadow him. Some of the limits, I complied with. I wanted him to succeed. For instance, I never wore attention-grabbing colors when we were in public. I also never wore heels because at five eight, I towered over his five-six frame. Those restrictions had become second nature, doable; the constant micromanaging—not so much. Then came the final straw: his lack of interest in having sex with me. That position—missionary, as I recalled from the three times we'd had sex in the last year—had been given to my replacement, his soon-to-be fiancée, Hannah. She was twenty-two, and only five foot two.

Of course, I had nothing against her height. My cry of foul play came from her having an affair with him while we were married. It takes two, and one was married, but she had only been the tip of his iceberg of treachery. His other mistresses I found out about after I filed for the divorce. Each one was a cut on my heart, pride, and confidence. I took the last bit of my ego I had left the day I found them together and left him.

Finishing up, I slipped on a nightgown and made a mental note to get new lingerie. I was about to plug my phone in to charge when I noticed a new text from Liz.

Liz: Marco contacted The Agency and they offered a screening appointment for tomorrow. I told them yes, sorry it's so fast, but once it's done you can go to the next available mixer. I can't go, but I promise you'll have a good time. The appointment is at 11 a.m. sharp. They send their own cars. It'll take a few hours. Thank me later.

I shook my head and smiled. That was Liz. She wasn't one to waste time if she could help it, but was I ready?

I sighed heavily and set my alarm for nine. Climbing into bed, I read on my Kindle for a while and then tried to masturbate. For the life of me, I couldn't get myself to climax. My mind went to the last time I tried to have sex with Patrick.

"Harder. Fuck me harder," I instructed. "Grab my hair."

Patrick huffed in exertion and pulled out of me. His body was covered in sweat. "What's your problem?"

I averted my eyes and moved onto my knees. "I just thought we'd try something different."

"What now?" he said in a condescending tone.

I bit my lip. "How about you hold my arms while you fuck me?"

"Stop saying that word," he said. "I am...we are having sex. You're just being difficult."

I sighed heavily. "I'm not trying to be."

He stretched out on his side, facing me. "Are you trying to make me hurt you?"

"No," I mumbled. "I just thought we could maybe spice things up a bit."

I let my hair fall over my face to avoid the disdain on his face, though it was unavoidable in his tone. "Spice by being rough? I'm not doing that! That's perverted."

My stomach churned. "You mean I'm perverted?"

"I didn't say that," he said, rubbing my back. "Come on, give me a break. I've been working hard all day."

I turned over on my back and opened my legs while he stretched out on top of me. He was back on autopilot, moving mechanically above me while I breathed in and waited until he cried out his climax. When he was done, he rolled over and kissed my head. "Did you come or do you need...?"

"I'm fine. It was great," I said with a forced lift to my voice. I waited until I heard his snoring then got up and went to my bathroom.

I pulled out my vibrator from the back of my vanity drawer and placed it against my clitoris. My eyes shut tight as I slipped away, imagining the faceless man of my fantasies fucking me. He was taking me hard, controlling me, owning me.

***

I tried to find out more about this agency before I went to my meeting, but my search online came back with nothing. Though my curiosity was thoroughly piqued, I understood my experience would more than likely be different than Liz's. After my frustrated attempt at masturbation, I wasn't up for spending more time without company.

If The Agency resulted in nothing more than meeting a man and having good sex instead of dates, I was still game. With that in mind, I climbed into the black Mercedes that arrived at 10:30 a.m. and went to my appointment. Given the weather, I chose a scoop-neck sweater, woolen slacks, and boots, though the car ride was warm and comfortable.

Their office turned out to be just a short ride away in one of the new modern buildings in Redmond. After some security checks, I went up to the eighth floor and over to the placard that read *The Agency* outside of suite 801. The interior was small and made up of mostly white wood and marble furnishings. Seated behind the reception desk was an older female with horn-rimmed glasses wearing a lab coat over a white shirt. She smiled at me in greeting and requested the card Liz had given me. Once she put it away, she handed me an iPad with a screen that said *Agency Member G. Ruiz Questionnaire* across it.

"Please fill this out to the best of your abilities," she instructed. "You'll be receiving a health and psychological screen. We're not here to judge, but the more honest you are, the easier it is to link you with like-minded partners. This includes if you are a book lover, art lover, whatever. Try to be as detailed and honest as possible so we'll be sure to find you the right match."

I sighed. I understood and appreciated the health screen for sexually transmitted diseases. I'd gotten one done after discovering the affair, and thankfully it had come back negative. However, I'd also been through marriage therapy, and I didn't enjoy or want to participate in counseling again. Even so, I agreed to it. "Sure." I glanced around the empty reception area to the side of the desk and saw only a couple of chairs. "Am I your first appointment?"

"You're the only person here besides our staff. We only make one appointment at a time for privacy reasons." She gestured to the corner of the room where one leather chair was available for me to sit.

"Good." I smiled.

"After your health exam, William, one of our counselors, will meet with you to clear up any last questions you may have."

I thanked her then sat down and scrolled through the screen. First was a non-disclosure agreement, followed by a section that asked me to select a standard set of attributes that attracted me physically. Further along, the questions became more specific.

Would you rather throw a party or attend it?

I shrugged.

Attend.

On a scale of 1-10, how would you rate yourself physically?

I grimaced. I hated that question. Too high, you're over the top; too low, you have low self-esteem.

Seven.

Choose 3 positives to describe yourself: adventurous, sexy, calm, fun, kind, creative, devoted, insightful, sweet, affectionate.

Hmm. Calm is boring. Kind and sweet is a pushover. Affectionate and devoted is desperate.

Creative, sexy, adventurous.

Choose 3 negatives to describe yourself: stubborn, high-maintenance, moody, demanding, uncertain, impulsive, compulsive, impatient, jealous, naughty.
Do not leave blank.

Impulsive, jealous (depends), naughty.

Going to spank me?

I laughed and moved on to the next question.

How many sexual partners have you had?

I sighed.

Three.

Is there a sexual position you don't like?

I snorted. I had no idea. My extensive experience included missionary and doggy style.

Don't know, try me.

Have you had more than one partner at a time and did you enjoy it?

Yes. I prefer two men at a time.

I laughed and went to remove it, but it wouldn't let me go backward.

Should I say something?

I glanced over at the receptionist, who was on the phone, but then decided to forget it. I'd just tell them later I was joking if asked.

From here on out, I'd be more focused when filling in the rest of my answers.

What is your active sexual life in years? How long and how often did you have sex?

I was in a relationship for seven years. We had sex three times a week the first year and progressively less over the years. We had sex three times the whole of the last year.

What is more important, physical attraction or personality?

I hesitated. The question was too vague. I had to be attracted to him, but I didn't want a wimp. I chose looks, but also wrote in the *Other* section.

I like a combination of both.

I laughed. I sure was making a tall order, but then looks were subjective. What attracts one person may not attract another. The next question went into more detail.

What turns you on more, being in control or giving up control?

I was used to being in control. I had run Patrick's campaigns, and now I ran my own company. I wasn't as experienced in the bedroom and wouldn't mind having a more dominant partner there. I clicked on *Other* and wrote a quick explanation in the box.

I run a business and wouldn't want to be controlled all the time. I would consider sexual control only.

Have you ever tried role-play, spanking, bondage, breath-play, watersports, scat, whips…?

The list went on, and most I'd have to look up, but for now my answer was easy.

No.

From the list above, which one piques your curiosity?

This was my moment. I could answer *No interest* or *Willing to try a few new things.* On the other hand, I didn't want to be thrown into the deep end. Therefore, I selected *Other* once again.

I don't like extreme humiliation or severe pain. I'm not ready for anything too far out of the mainstream.

After all, you must walk before you run. I doubted there would ever be such a match that would get me to entertain surrendering so much of myself.

How do you feel about enclosed spaces?

I don't mind.

How do you feel about being restrained?

I paused at that one. Where on the spectrum did I fall? Better to be cautious.

I wouldn't be a match for anyone into anything extreme. That means not past silk scarves on my wrists.

Have you watched porn or read erotica?

I smirked. Hasn't everyone? It then went into detail on how much I read, how often, and what turned me on. I didn't believe myself to be dirty, but I didn't know what kind of partner I would attract with these answers. My mind wrestled with my honesty, but I answered close to the truth.

Often.

Are you embarrassed by these questions?

I laughed a little.

Yes.

I completed the rest of the questions and handed over the iPad. A staff member took me back to a physical exam room for a health screen for drugs and sexually transmitted diseases. The screen included a request for me to list all forms of birth control used in the present and past. I had been on the pill since I was seventeen and had done a physical during my divorce, but they were adamant about doing their own. I appreciated their care toward clients' health, sexual and otherwise, and complied. Then I was taken next door to a small dimly lit office with two overstuffed cushioned chairs. William, an older male in a white lab coat and designer slacks, greeted me before I took a seat. "How did you find our process?" he asked.

"A bit more detailed than I expected," I admitted.

He tilted his head. "You expected something else?"

"No, not really. I only heard about The Agency yesterday," I said. "From my friend."

The skin around his eyes crinkled. "Must have been some friend. It's rare we allow a meeting so quickly. Perhaps I should explain what we are first. At its core, The Agency is a matchmaking service. Some come for relationships, lifestyle changes, fantasies, revelations, revitalizations," he said. "What about you?"

I nervously ran my hands down my arms before returning them to my lap. "I was hoping to meet someone new—a date perhaps."

"A new friend-lover?" he asked.

I nodded. "I'd say a new friend-lover is close to what I'm looking for. I'm not looking to marry again. I'm only recently divorced."

He nodded. "You don't have to answer that definitively now. Your answers today will help us populate the mixer with matches suitable for you."

"That must take time," I said. "No one mentioned the cost of this service."

"If you received a card, someone has paid the fee on your behalf," he explained.

I shook my head. "No, a friend gave me hers."

He picked up a pad and barely glanced down at the screen. "There is nothing outstanding, no need to worry. Now, do you have any other questions?"

I shrugged. "I don't right now, but I may have some later. This all seems well organized, but besides the health check and psych screening, I don't see how your company is different than any of the other matchmaking companies out there."

"The Agency is different—better," he replied. "We haven't had any disappointed clients."

I raised my brows, doubtful. There was no way you could please everyone, but why argue?

He closed my file and gestured toward the door.

"That's it?" I asked.

"Yes. The questionnaire and exam will tell us everything we need to know. You'll hear from us soon."

I shook his hand and left. The veil of mystery hadn't been lifted, and I was still curious about how The Agency would match me and just what I'd gotten myself into.

***

I returned home and unpacked a few boxes before giving up and driving over to the local gym for some cardio and toning. I hadn't been for a while and found that I was exhausted after the first twenty minutes. I pressed on for the full fifty minutes I had planned. Afterward, I rewarded myself with a small latte at the café next door. The whole time, I kept wondering about my experience at The Agency. How long would it take for them to process my information? Who had paid the fee for me? Liz? With the car, complete physical, and lab work, it went beyond what I'd consider a reasonable holiday gift. It made me uneasy. I planned to discuss it with Liz and cover the cost of whatever fees she had paid for my membership.

When I arrived home, there was a floral delivery van parked out front. I raised my brows. Christmas gift from a friend?

Pulling into the driveway, I was met by a delivery man on my porch. Once I got the door open, I cleared off a space on the table and he came in with twenty-four long-stem white roses in a crystal vase with a Tiffany's bow. He refused the tip and handed me an elaborately crafted embossed card. In it was a gift certificate for a full-day treatment at Spa Noir along with a beautiful invitation.

You're invited to a private party tomorrow
night at
Westbrook Estate on Mercer Island
A limousine will pick you up at 9:00 p.m.
Dress: Formal
RSVP if you are not available
Please present invitation as admittance

I stared down at the invitation and frowned. *Tomorrow?* That was a bit too quick for me. It left little time for introspection. I'd have to decide now whether to attend, not to mention get my hair done and shop for something to wear. I wasn't sure what to do and thought advice from Liz would settle whatever nerves I had. She answered on the second ring and I told her about the invitation and the fee having been paid. "Is this a Christmas gift?"

"I didn't have to pay either, but I was told they have a lot of rich clientele that want to

48

make sure the participants meet their requirements."

What she said made sense, but it still didn't sit right with me.

"I'm glad it's fast so you can't change your mind," she said in a light tone and laughed. "The mixer I went to was in downtown Seattle. I suppose they hold them at different places. Do you know who the host is?"

"It just says 'Westbrook Estate on Mercer Island'. I don't know, I'd have liked to be more informed," I said, picking up my iPad and going into the kitchen. I took a seat at one of the four stools I had positioned around the laminate kitchen island and scrolled for the number of the spa.

"You'll be fine," she said. "There will be plenty of men and women there to meet and you can always leave, but I hope you meet someone—wait, did you say Westbrook?"

"Yup, I did." I bit into my lip. "Was that supposed to be a secret?"

"I don't think so," she replied. "Even if someone knew about the party, they wouldn't just be able to walk in. Besides, I gave you the card."

"True," I agreed. "Who do you think the host could be?"

"You said Westbrook on Mercer Island, right? That could only be the architect, Dane Westbrook," she said. "He was the one you asked about at the restaurant."

I grinned, remembering how incredibly good-looking he was. "What do you know about him?"

"Not much, I'm afraid. He and his friends are quite the mystery," she said. "Honestly, I didn't even know he hosted parties. Every mixer is custom to profiles. I've never been to a party he attended, but Marco says some are exclusive. Could it be something you wrote on your questionnaire?"

"I honestly don't have a clue," I said. "But if The Agency has attractive men like him, I'm definitely interested, at least for a night or two."

"You're bad." She laughed with me. "You must tell me what happens."

"Just like you shared your dates with Marco?" I said as I poured a glass of water from the dispenser in the refrigerator.

She giggled. "Well, I didn't want to break the spell. He's been so...sweet to me. God, I'm like a teenager in love here."

I bit my cheek. I wanted her to be cautious, but it was so good to hear her joy that I didn't want to ruin it. "Just be careful," I told her.

"I am," she said. "But now that I'm alone, I don't see any reason to not try something new. Now that you're single, you don't have to settle. You don't need to depend on a man for financial security. You have your business, and your parents' estate too—unless Patrick got alimony?"

I grimaced. "He tried, but his affair with Hannah put a wrench in his alimony plan— although I wouldn't put it past him to keep his lawyers sniffing around for a way to get more money from me, the slimy bastards." We bashed him a bit and I smiled when I hung up.

Almost immediately, the phone rang again. This time Patrick's name flashed on the screen.

"Hello, Gia," he said in a cheery voice.

"What do you want?" I asked. My voice wasn't fake; it was downright snippy.

"We can be pleasant even if we are divorced," he said in his most polite tone. "I was wondering if you remembered the contacts in Senator Ellis's office."

I rolled my eyes. Of course he was calling because he needed to use me for help with his campaign. I was the one who'd handled all the pesky details he never seemed to make time for. *Too busy cheating.* Call it a moment of holiday mercy, but I ran through a contact list off the top of my head.

"See, I knew you would know," he said. "You know...now that we're divorced, I was wondering if you could give Hannah some pointers on fundraising?"

I smirked. Had hell frozen over? Had he completely lost his mind? "We're not friends anymore, Patrick. I don't want you calling me. You replaced me, now work with your replacement."

"We both know it wasn't that simple," he said. "You checked out of this marriage, spending all your time on that little project—"

"The little project you and your slimy lawyers are trying to get a hold of," I said tersely. My little project had turned lucrative over the years, growing well beyond his original investment.

"No, I invested, and it's communal property from the time we were married. We contracted our agreement. I agreed to change, and you agreed to be helpful," he said in a sharp tone. That voice had once been used to keep me in line, but now that was totally not going to happen. While my family had money and connections, my father wouldn't give me a startup loan, wanting me to stay away from business. In the end, we had agreed to use a percentage of Patrick's salary for the initial funding for Perfetto, and even after replacing his investment, he still found a way to bring it up to get something from me.

"No. I agreed not to do anything that would jeopardize your election." I drew in a breath. "Such as telling them about how your affair with Hannah came about."

He coughed. "We both agreed not to discuss Hannah. She is being introduced as my new public relations consultant, not my girlfriend. I may have had relations with Hannah earlier than one would expect, but we were not together until after the separation."

"Liar," I snipped. This was his typical song and dance, anything to avoid telling the truth. "You fucked her on our bed."

"The way it all happened was a mistake," he said, and it was the closest he'd ever come to admitting his affair. "When was the last time you wanted to have sex with me?"

My lips twisted. "Are you really trying to blame me for your cheating? I'm hanging up."

"Wait, please," he said quickly, his tone rapidly becoming civil again. "We're past arguing...I just wanted to find out some information."

I sighed. "You have the notebooks I kept. They are very detailed," I replied. "I'm sure you must have them because I can't find them."

"You used codes," he said tersely. "If you could tell me and maybe introduce—"

I twisted my mouth. "That's never going to happen."

"After all these years, you can't be this cruel."

My mouth went dry. Seriously? This was just going around in circles. I decided to take another route. "From what I've heard, Hannah's father is well connected."

"He's being a hard ass," he griped. "He wants me to work on it myself—"

I smiled wickedly. *Too fucking bad.* "I like his thinking. You should work on it yourself. I've got to go."

"Christ, Gia, don't be a bitch."

I hung up and made plans for The Agency's mixer.

I was ready for a change, whatever that happened to be.

CHAPTER THREE

The Spa Noir package was a full day that included a facial, manicure, pedicure, and wax, and Astrid came along for a holiday break. We both found the pampering divine, and afterward, we went dress shopping. The red and black pumps I'd ordered had arrived by express carrier and went well with the cocktail dress we found at Nordstrom, with its Italian lace, floral print, V-neckline, and sheer georgette material.

"You look stunning," Astrid said after I added a light sheer powder and finished off my makeup with run-free mascara and the crimson lipstick. The makeup was strictly Perfetto, of course. "You'll have them fighting over you."

I laughed and brushed through my long hair, which I was letting hang free down my back in curls. "Maybe one or two of them," I joked back.

Outwardly, I felt confident in my appearance, but inside, I was a bundle of nerves. Who would I meet? What if I didn't meet anyone I wanted to date?

"Really Gia, I was surprised you took Liz up on her offer to go through a match service," she said, handing me my ruby and black pearl earrings. "What was the name of it again?"

"The Agency," I said as my phone beeped. I checked the message and found it was the driver. "The car service is here."

"That's an odd name for a company," Astrid said, buttoning up her coat. "The Agency could be anything, but if Liz is happy, it can't be all that bad."

I hugged her. "Thank you for coming with me today. It made me less nervous, but now I've run out of time and I'm not sure I'm ready—"

"You'll be fine," she said. "Quit worrying. Just go have fun." We hugged each other and left in two different directions. Astrid's would take her back to her little family, while mine...well, who knew where it would take me?

The drive over to Mercer Island didn't take long from where I lived in Bellevue. Visibility was limited with the night sky and snowfall, but with the headlights of the limousine, I could make out rows of landscaped poplar trees and gates to contemporary mansions. The car stopped at one of the stone and iron gates. This one was open with a row of exterior lantern lights. A female hostess in a winter coat and suit opened the door and helped me onto the sandstone driveway, up to a wide staircase that had two Tuscan columns next to the large windows and door at the entry. There, another host was waiting to take my coat, and after consulting his list, he provided me with a small red ribbon corsage to wear at my wrist.

"What's this for?" I asked.

He smiled. "Identification. This is your first mixer?"

"Yes," I said.

"This is a pheromone mist. It's non-toxic, hypoallergenic, and unscented." He sprayed my neck.

"We'll try that too." A handsome man dressed in a tuxedo appeared at my side. He had short blond hair with thin-framed square glasses and a wide grin. He was holding the hand of a smiling brunette. She was short and curvy with shoulder-length hair, and she was dressed in a black sequined mini-dress and stilettos. Her big brown eyes glimpsed me before settling back on him. "I'm Bradley, and this is Sophie. You are?"

"Gia," I said and took his hand then let go first. "Nice to meet you." When I went to shake Sophie's hand, I was surprised to find a green corsage around her wrist. That was when I noticed Bradley had a green bow around the red rose pinned to his collar. I wondered what the colors meant.

Before I could ask, he said, "Come with us. I'll get the two of you drinks. Wine okay with you?"

I smiled and took them up on their offer. "Red, please. Thank you."

Following them past the foyer and double marble and mahogany staircase, we arrived at a spacious living room where a diverse group of men and women congregated on seats and stood chatting. The room itself contained a tasteful mix of antiques and modern furnishings, including a large fireplace, bronze sculptures, and framed renaissance artwork that worked for the space. The overall assembly was beautiful, including the Italian marble and stone on the floor, the exposed wooden beams along the vaulted ceilings, and the carved wooden paneling. A row of windows the length of the room provided a view out to Lake Washington, and I suspected Dane Westbrook had a view of Mount Rainer during the day. The place was wonderful.

Sophie and I settled in at the bar while Bradley ordered drinks for us. The men were mostly in tuxedos or designer suits, the women in various cocktail dresses. The Agency hadn't disappointed in options—the gathering was entirely made up of attractive people. Although none of the men caught my eye at first glance, I didn't rule any of them out either.

"Do you come to mixers often?" I asked Sophie.

"Not often," she responded. "I came to get my mind off losing my job—"

"Now, now, Sophie, we agreed this night is for us to have fun," Bradley said then kissed her cheek. "You'll have something new before you know it."

"Yes, I will," she said, staring after Bradley as he went to collect our drinks. "Bradley and I come occasionally to meet new people."

I lifted my brow curiously. "Oh, I assumed you were—"

"Together," she finished for me and nodded. "We are. We have an open relationship."

"Oh," was all I could think to say.

Bradley returned and handed me my glass. "What's our topic?" he asked, his green eyes shifting between the two of us.

"Our open relationship," she said, touching his arm.

He chuckled and kissed her cheek. "That came up quick."

"I didn't ask," I clarified politely. "Sophie mentioned it."

"Now that we're on the subject," he said, not missing a beat, "what are your thoughts on open relationships, Gia?"

My lips parted. I didn't know what to say right on the spot, but since they were asking, I thought it was best to go with honesty. "I don't have many thoughts on the subject. I believe I'm open-minded regarding whatever anyone chooses to do that's right for them. As for myself, I'd be too jealous."

"That's what we had thought previously," Sophie said. "But sex for most species on earth isn't monogamous. We all have different attractions. It's only natural to want to copulate with others, but real intimacy is beyond sex."

I shrugged my shoulders. *Whatever gets you through the night.* "Okay."

"You don't have to agree, of course," Bradley said. "It's whatever you're comfortable with." He placed his arm around Sophie's waist, and she leaned into him then kissed him deeply.

I took a sip of my wine and tried not to stare. They were being affectionate while simultaneously talking about sharing each other. I didn't understand the concept, and I liked that they didn't try to get me to. When they came up for air and returned to our conversation, I said, "I can't really speak on open relationships. I'm recently divorced, and this is my first time getting back out there. I feel like I need training wheels."

"Or you need a good teacher," said a man's voice, smooth as silk behind me. I turned around as he came closer, and I recognized him at once: Dane Westbrook. He stood close to six-two, and instead of a tuxedo, he wore a designer black suit and dark gray shirt that contrasted with his pale gray eyes as they met my light brown gaze.

"Dane," Bradley said, greeting him warmly with a handshake and a clasp on his broad shoulder.

"You look lovely tonight, Sophie," Dane said, moving on to her. He kissed her cheeks, causing her to blush pink, which made me curious. Had he been a part of their open relationship?

It wasn't my business, but when it was my turn and I stood under his shrewd gaze, I had to fight hard to school my face into passivity or he'd get my version of the golden look—wide welcoming eyes and a grin that spreads from ear to ear. It was a look reserved for a very short list of fantasy men. It was a look that, when he saw it, would let him know he wouldn't have to try to win me because he already had me. *I would go to bed with him.*

Just the thought brought heat to my face and made my breaths come faster. It was unnerving, but so was Dane Westbrook. He was positively breathtaking. I'd always had a thing for men with dark hair. His was coiffured back in waves that tapered neatly just above his collar. His bone structure was elegant, his jaw freshly shaven. His full lips turned up into a broad smile and revealed an even set of white teeth.

He lifted my hand to his mouth and placed a soft kiss on the back of it. I felt a tingle go through me at the contact.

"Gia Ruiz," he said, surprising me by knowing my name without introduction. "I received a call from The Agency to invite you. I'm glad you were able to join us on such short notice."

"I was totally free," I said.

His lip twitched and my face warmed. *God, why did I say that? Sounds thirsty. Tone it down.*

I straightened my shoulders. "Thank you for the invitation. You have a lovely home."

"Thank you," he said. His large hand took my elbow. It was warm and firm, slightly calloused, like he worked with his hands. "How about we talk and let Bradley and Sophie have a chance to mingle? Perhaps I can introduce you around."

"He'll introduce, but he's not participating," Bradley said. His tone was light, but the look between them wasn't.

"He's right about that," Dane said evenly. "I'm hosting the mixer tonight. I'm here to help you find a match, not be one."

I turned my head to hide the disappointment that arose within me, and my eyes widened in surprise as his hand slipped around my waist and rested on my lower back. It felt so natural that I didn't move away.

Bradley's eyes shifted between us, and a small smile formed on his lips. "Nice to meet you, Gia. Hope to see you again."

Dane moved us over to an available spot on one of the leather couches. He got the attention of a hostess and ordered a scotch for himself.

I returned my wine glass and declined another. "So, why get involved if you're not..."

"Looking for a match?" he finished for me. "I'm a partner in the company, and part of our agreement is to host parties. I say I'm not interested, but perhaps I'm jaded. To be honest, I doubt I'd find a woman that could handle my proclivities."

There was a twinkle in his eyes and amusement in his voice, which made me wonder if he meant what he said. If he did, I understood being jaded from my divorce, but he, like me, was there, so he must have had some sort of optimistic streak.

"What about yourself?" he asked, sipping his drink.

"I'm recently divorced," I replied candidly. "I'm not so sure about finding a match, but I'd like to find a date." Date sounded better than *I'm looking for sex*, and why not expand my horizons? I hadn't had much experience with either. I'd dated in college, but I became Patrick's girlfriend my sophomore year, and he was one of the few men I ever had sex with.

"We have that in common. I got divorced, but in my early twenties," he replied. "I'm thirty-four now. May I ask how old you are?"

"Twenty-eight," I answered.

He tilted his head and grinned. "You look different than the first time I saw you."

"At the restaurant in Seattle," I offered. "I was meeting my friend Liz and her new boyfriend. I think you know him...Marco?"

His eyes flashed. "You met him?"

My lips parted. "No, I didn't."

He sighed and gave a nod. His reaction tipped me off that he wasn't much of a fan of

Marco's, so I changed our conversation back to where he had headed it. His mentioning having met me before had me intrigued. "So, where did you first see me?"

"It was at the housing initiative fundraiser last year," he replied. "I'm on the board, and I also design and build homes for families in need. You were with your husband at the time. I remember you because you were standing off to the side."

"My usual method for blending into the background," I said lightly, though it had irritated me at the time to be in the back where Patrick had wanted me—out of his spotlight. Getting involved in the housing initiative had been my idea, and Patrick had only agreed because of the photo op on a high-profile policy issue.

"You didn't blend in," he said. "I don't think it's possible for you to do anything but stand out."

I lowered my eyes and grinned. "I didn't know you were there."

His gaze was intense as it bore into mine, so much so that I turned my head, but I didn't want him to go. "So, you're an architect. Did you design this house?"

He nodded and shared about his work as an architect and a sculptor. "I've done some of the artwork on display here. Over there is Incubus Nymph." He pointed to the bronze image of the devil and a nude female nymph. The more he spoke, the more I didn't want him to stop, but then he grew quiet and had someone take his glass away.

"They're beautiful," I enthused. "I'd love to get a remodel on my new place one day."

"We're available for assessments," he said. "Even if you don't go with my company, I can give you some ideas on strengths and what would need remodeling."

I smiled. "I'd love that."

"Now tell me about your work," he said, and I launched into a bit about Perfetto. He stared at me like every word out of my mouth was interesting and I had his full attention, so focused and close that I found a nervous energy rushing through me as I talked about the company. My nervousness only intensified when he moved closer on the seat. Our thighs were touching, and a charge kindled at the point of contact. My pulse sped up and my breath quickened. It was terribly, sensually distracting.

I thought I detected a flicker of interest in his eyes as they slid downward. It caused a tingling low in my body that had me glancing away due to my inability to hide how much I welcomed his interest in me. Then he suddenly stood and took my hands to help me stand.

"I've forgotten my manners," he apologized. "I should be introducing you around. In fact, I know someone I think you have a lot in common with."

I smirked. Was he serious? I didn't know what to make of it, but I was there to meet someone new and thus let him lead me over to a good-looking man built like an athlete. His hair was wheat blond and gelled back. "Gia, this is Michael Hertzog. His company designed the pheromone spray we used tonight."

Michael smiled warmly at me. "Nice to meet you."

"Likewise," I said with a tight smile.

Dane moved away from us and I got into a conversation with Michael about his company and my own. He was interesting and we found we had much in common, but there wasn't an initial spark of attraction, nothing like I had experienced with Dane.

Dane...

My eyes couldn't help but roam the room to find him, and I wasn't the only one. His presence was compelling. Everywhere he stopped in the room, he was given undivided attention. It could have been because he gave off an air of authority and had the appearance of someone who would demand instant obedience. It could have been the confident way he carried himself. He radiated a masculine force that drew you in. He was like an irresistible beacon, and I couldn't stop my eyes from scanning the room to find him. When I gave in to the impulse to see him, I found him looking my way, and a sensuous light seemed to pass between us before I forced myself back into the conversation at hand. Even so, my interest was conflicted. I wanted more time with Dane.

As a group of guests came over to speak with Michael, I took the chance to excuse myself for a trip to the bathroom with a promise to return afterward. There was a balcony, and I hoped it was available so I could go outside for a few minutes. I wanted a chance to gather my thoughts to decide what I wanted to do. I understood why I had been brought there. Most of the men I met had the same background as I did, a shared business and industry mindset. They were all complimentary and cautious and, for a lack of a better description, like me. So why was I disappointed?

That was the million-dollar question I thought about after a staff member directed me up the stairs, which I quickly ascended. It was dark except for the light coming from the top of a deep gold velvet curtain that was tastefully draped across the entryway at the end. Lively music was coming from the other side. Now that was the kind of party I was interested in.

Another host stood outside of it and met me on approach as I made my way farther down the hall. "You don't have the clearance to be up here." He eyed my ribbon. "What are you searching for?"

"The bathroom," I replied, hesitating. "But...is that another part of the party?"

He hesitated too. "It's part of the party, but this one is for green members. Sorry. The restroom is over there." He gestured toward a large oak door across from where I stood. I nodded and went in. After I finished and washed my hands, I freshened up my makeup. While I wasn't excited about returning to the mixer downstairs, I reminded myself that I wasn't looking for a love match. I was looking for a start, and dating someone would be a new beginning. With that in mind, I walked out the door.

The music down the hall had mellowed, but I was still curious about what was going on behind the curtain. The host had stepped away, and I saw my chance. I quickly plucked off the red flower from my corsage and walked down the hall. I pulled back the soft fabric and stepped inside. The double doors were closed but unlocked, and I made it a good foot inside before I froze.

There was a completely different kind of party going on in here and while I knew I shouldn't have been there, I couldn't get my feet to turn and walk away. I was instantaneously absorbed.

I'd seen porn on the computer before, but nothing like the live sexual orgy I was witnessing now. The lights were soft, but there was no hiding what was going on in the suite: a group of men and women in various stages of undress kissing, touching, and stroking each other. In the center of the room was one of the largest four-poster beds I'd ever seen, and several people were having sex on it. Some couples were on top of each other, others performing oral on a third partner. It was hard to look away from the bed, but what caught my eye among the groups on the side was Sophie. She was standing in front of Bradley, her naked body writhing in his arms as he massaged her breasts, and that wasn't all that was happening. Another man was on his knees between her thighs, orally pleasuring her, and I couldn't look away. It was as if a fantasy had been plucked from my mind. My body heated as my breathing got shallow. I could feel my arousal between my thighs. A woman who had stood near me, just watching, went over to them, and Bradley let go of Sophie and started kissing her.

While I was completely beguiled by the openly hedonistic sex show, I hadn't realized a man had come to stand next to me until he leaned down to my ear and whispered, "You like watching the man rubbing her tits while the other man eats her pussy?" His voice was a deep, sultry caress. I glanced to the side once, then again. The man stood tall in a well-tailored tuxedo. The reflective lights glimmered over his handsome face, highlighting the angles of the elegant ridges of his cheekbones. His bright blue eyes and white smile were also hard to miss, especially with him leaning closer to me.

I let my hair cover my flushed face as I sucked in air. My thighs clenched together. "I...I didn't mean to stare." I was tongue-tied. Did he know I shouldn't be in there?

"They want you to stare," the man said. "They want to turn you on. You can touch yourself too. No one will care."

A look around the room confirmed his assessment. No one was watching me. Everyone in the room was caught up in their own pleasure.

He went behind me and moved his body flush up against mine. I inhaled his cologne, a pleasing cedar wood and herb mix. He had me so close that I could feel his muscles ripple under his shirt, his cock full and erect as it pressed against my buttocks. He was like a strong solid force. I waited for my brain to kick in and get me out the door, but my feet felt rooted. I didn't want to go. The stranger was right—I wanted to stay. I wanted to touch myself.

The sound of Sophie's ecstatic cry at her climax filled my ears and my eyes were back on the scene playing out before me. Bradley lowered his pants behind Sophie, who bent over at the waist. The other man with them stood and took out his cock then guided it into her mouth.

"Go on, touch your pussy. I know you're wet," he purred into my ear. "Or do you need help? I'd be happy to get you started."

My pulse jumped in my throat as heat filled my body. I was turned on by his words and I was tempted to do it, but I couldn't.

Could I? I mean who was he?

"I shouldn't...I don't even know you." My words came out breathy. I was conflicted.

"This must be your first time. I'm Elliott, one of the hosts in this room. In here, you can do whatever you want." His strong hand slid around my waist. I could feel the brush of his

79

lips next to my ear as he whispered, "In here, you don't need to know me. You just need to feel. You give and receive pleasure freely. I want to stroke your pussy and feel you come. Let me make you come."

I wavered, not consenting or declining. Although I wanted to come more than my next breath, my conscience screamed that I didn't know who he was, and I wasn't in the habit of letting strangers touch me intimately. It was improper, immoral, not me—but the sexually charged air in the room and having his strong arms around me was incredibly enticing. It was a temptation I didn't necessarily want to turn down. Still, something got the better of me. "I shouldn't be in here. This is a mistake." Even so, I didn't move away. I was totally captivated.

"You're still here. I'd say it's a choice." He pressed his mouth to my neck and a moan escaped my lips. He kept a hold of me. My body was on fire with need and want. His hands felt the hard, sensitive points of my nipples through the top of my dress. The more he touched them, the more my mind explained away what I was doing. *It's just touching. I'm not having sex.*

A moan left my lips as I arched into his touch, and he continued to knead me through the fabric. "You smell delicious," he whispered. "Are you ready for me to feel your pussy?" I gasped as he slid his hands down to my hips.

"Elliott, stop what you're doing right now. She's a part of our red mixer." Dane's voice broke through, his tone sharp and commanding.

Oh no. My awareness came back as blood rushed to my face. *What have I done?* I felt I had been caught doing something I shouldn't, though Dane had no claim over me. Still, I couldn't bring myself to look at him.

Elliott kept me in his arms, seemingly unaffected by Dane's appearance. "She didn't stop me. She wants to be touched. I know she's wet. Feel her, Dane."

I flushed and closed my thighs together to try to quench the aching need that pulsed there. Oh, did I ever want Dane to touch me, but Elliott telling Dane to do so embarrassed me.

I finally pushed Elliott's hands away and he stepped back.

"Did you invite Elliott to touch you, Gia?" Dane asked. His manner was neutral.

I kept my gaze anywhere but him. "Not exactly, but I didn't move or tell him to stop. I permitted him to it," I admitted. I was enjoying it, though he must have thought I was a terrible slut.

"When you come in here, you're ready and willing to have sex," Elliott said. "Doesn't she know that?"

"She doesn't." He looked at my wrist where the red corsage was missing.

I bit my lip. "I didn't think I needed it for the whole night."

Elliott frowned. "I can't be expected to be looking at wrists all the time, and I can't do anything if she chose to remove it. She came in and stayed, and she even admitted she went along with what we did."

"Even so, she didn't know much about this mixer," Dane pointed out. "Now that she understands what's going on, she would need to consent to staying," Dane said as he touched my arm. "Honestly, Elliott meant no harm."

"I know. I removed my flower. I was just as involved…" If Dane hadn't appeared, I'd have let Elliott touch me. I *wanted* him to. I turned my head.

Dane's fingers slid under my chin and tilted my face up to his. My breath hitched. His light gray eyes were like silver lightning in their intensity as our gazes locked together. His expression was far from negative. I thought he might have even been intrigued.

"Forget convictions, there are no judgments here," he said. "There is nothing wrong with wanting to be touched. Do you want me to allow Elliott to stroke your pussy until you come?"

My mouth went dry and I shifted on my feet. His words were blunt, and they turned me on. His invitation was a passionate challenge, hard to resist. It touched that ache deep inside of me that longed to be touched again. "I don't even know him. It happened fast and I...I'm sorry."

I closed my eyes. I didn't want him to see any more of what I was thinking.

"Look at me," he said. His tone was gentle though authoritative.

I did. My pulse jumped in my throat.

"You have no reason to be sorry," he said. "If you hesitate to continue because of me, don't. I want you to. It would turn me on immensely for the two of us to make you come, but I need to hear the truth from you. Tell me."

I felt swollen between my legs. "I did...I do want to, but..."

I was too far gone to pass up his illicit offer. It had been ages since I'd been touched at all, and two men touching me was stepping well out of my comfort zone. This was more than I could imagine for myself. If I had, Dane would have been my choice. I'd had an attraction for him from the start.

Dane lifted my face up and let me see the licentious force on his own. "You want me to touch you too."

I nodded slowly. The thought of Dane touching me tightened things low in my body. I took in a shallow breath and glanced around us.

"Too public?" he said. "We'll compromise."

"This time," Elliott said, amused.

I blinked rapidly. This time? There wasn't going to be a next time. This was one-time-only for me. Even so, I could barely form a thought on what to do next.

He took my hand and instead of leading me out of the room, he moved us farther away from the bed and into a dimly lit corner. It wasn't exactly private, but it was away from the rest of the people.

"I want to see her whole body," Elliott said. He moved his hands toward the zipper on my dress.

My eyes darted around and I tensed at the very idea. "I don't want to take off my dress."

"She's not ready to be naked," Dane said, understanding. He ran his hand down my arm and I let out a ragged breath. He then turned me to face away from him and wrapped his arms around me. His warmth encircled me. His thick erection against my buttocks was distracting, but he didn't grind up against me, just kept me close. "Tell us again."

I stood there quietly for a few moments. Dane wasn't rushing. I got the impression he would stop touching me if I asked him to, even as far as we had gone. I had control, and I also had to make my choice be known. It was my desire, my desperate need to be touched intimately again, and with the intensity of the moment and the sounds of pleasure all around me, I had but one answer.

"Please...touch me," I whispered, giving voice to my plea.

"Good," he said with pleasure in his voice. He pressed a kiss to my neck then slowly lifted the end of my dress to the tops of my thighs. "Elliott, take her panties off."

Elliott didn't hesitate to reach under my dress and slide the lace down my legs, leaving me in thigh-highs. Goose bumps broke out across my skin in excitement as the front of my body was exposed.

Dane's hands gripped my thighs and pulled my legs apart, exposing me to Elliott, who remained on his knees, staring at me. I took in short breaths as I heated more. I squirmed back against Dane. My breasts felt achy and heavy, my pussy hot and swollen. Dane's hand went down to the top of my mound and stroked my skin. "So soft."

I squirmed and waited for him to move his hand lower, but he held me firmly in place.

I whimpered.

"Soon," Dane soothed.

Elliott leaned in and let his lips brush high on my thigh. I shivered and moaned as Elliot's fingers slid across my slit. My clit throbbed as he opened me wider.

Elliott groaned. "She's so beautiful and ripe, Dane. I want to suck your pussy, Gia. Just say the word." His breath was warm and close to my body. I wanted to feel it, but it was a step too far for me.

I tensed in Dane's arms at the thought, but didn't answer. This was one thing Patrick hadn't done, and he'd made me feel filthy for even wanting it.

"Don't worry," Dane said, again pressing his lips softly against my neck. "That's too much for her tonight," he said to Elliott. "Besides, I expect regret will come soon. We'll only make her come, like we said."

Elliott sighed noisily. "Regret is a waste."

"Relax, Gia," Dane said. The tips of his fingers grazed my throbbing clit. "So hot and wet...she's going to come fast." I moaned and protested as he moved his hand back to my mound. Then Elliot's hand caressed between my thighs and I cried out. His fingers slid across my clit and lower until he reached my entrance. My breaths became pants as my heart pounded. It felt so good.

Dane inhaled sharply as he stared down at Elliott's hand teasing the wetness before pushing two fingers inside of me. My inner walls gripped, pulling him farther in. "Fuck, she's tight." He brushed his lips at the top of my thigh. "You feel amazing."

I squeezed my eyes shut and panted as Elliott pumped two of his fingers into me. His thumb stroked over my clit, my body held firmly in Dane's embrace. His breath was as warm and fast as mine, and Elliott's fingers expertly found the spot inside that had me writhing and panting.

I was going to come hard, but I was climbing too quickly. I fought to hold back as I didn't want to come down from the intensity of the pleasure. I didn't want it to end, but the sensation was too pleasurable, too powerful.

"Let go, Gia," Dane growled commandingly.

I couldn't hold on. "Oh God," I cried out, convulsing around Elliott's fingers.

"Fuck, that's hot," Elliott groaned.

Dane hugged me to him as Elliott continued to stroke my pussy, prolonging my climax until I calmed. They both noticed the stiffening in my body and let me go. Out of the warmth of Dane's arms, I felt cold.

I yanked the front of my dress down and turned away from them. "I can't believe I just did that."

Elliott cursed. "You did and you loved it."

I looked away. "This is not me...normally I would never have let two men touch me like that, here in public..."

"See, Dane?" he said. "This is exactly why I can't stand tourists."

As discreetly as I could, I put on my underwear and fixed my dress. Dane went further and adjusted the end of my dress more, smoothing it in place. "There's no judgment. We enjoyed pleasuring you, Gia."

I shook my head. Maybe no judgment from Dane, but it was clear Elliott had an opinion. "I'm not...this isn't me. I'm going home."

I pushed them both away as I rushed down the staircase and down the hallway until I found a hostess and requested to leave. My orgasm still surged through me, my desire still hoping and yearning for more, but I couldn't stay after what I'd done and had let them do to me.

"Gia, you're leaving?" I looked up to find one of the men I had been speaking to. "I went to look for you, but they closed off upstairs. I had hoped you'd be interested in having dinner together next week."

I lowered my eyelids. How would he feel about dating me if he knew what I'd just done upstairs with two men? "I've decided I'm not ready for any of this."

"All right. I understand," he said. I didn't miss the disappointment in his voice. "Can I at least call you?"

My smile tightened. I didn't want him to call, but he continued to stand there, and my mind tried to conjure up a polite excuse as I put on my coat, one of the staff holding it out for me.

"Gia, I'd like to speak with you before you go." Dane's rich deep voice rang out from behind us, and my pulse jumped as he placed his arm firmly around my waist. My breath hitched as a tingling sensation arose between my thighs, reminding me once again how it had felt in his arms when I climaxed with him and his friend.

"I'm tired. Perhaps another time," I whispered. I couldn't stop the breathlessness of my voice, or the way my body trembled when his hand brushed low on my abdomen as he removed my coat. The inescapable heat between us intensified, making me aroused, unnerved.

"You're already here," he said then took my hand. "Come with me."

CHAPTER FOUR

"Where are you taking me?" Excitement coursed through my body as Dane maintained his possession of me.

"To talk," he said calmly as he led me through the back of his house. I didn't understand what he wanted from me now. My idea of leaving the mixer early would have given him and all that had happened the distance and discretion it needed.

Even though he had me, I knew I could leave if I wanted to go. He wasn't pulling or dragging me, though going along with him had ended my chance at a quick escape from what I had done with him and his friend. Doing something so public was risky. Could I risk my

AMÉLIE S. DUNCAN

reputation and the future of Perfetto with my recklessness? I tried to put it out of my mind.

Dane opened the door and turned on the lights. I could see it was a studio with a few drafting tables, design boards, and workstations. It also appeared to be a mini apartment with a kitchen, brown leather couches, and throws. He motioned for me to take a seat then poured us drinks, handing me a glass of wine before sitting in the chair across from me.

He took a sip from his glass of dark liquor before meeting my eyes, and when he did, something pulled my attention to him. I wasn't sure if it was the unabashed weight of his gaze when he looked at me or the sexual magnetism emanating from him that made his stare unnerving, but the silence bothered me. I cleared my throat and stated the obvious, though it came out more abrupt than I meant it to. "Are we just going to sit here staring at each other?"

"I thought you needed a minute to collect yourself," he said, his full lips spreading into an amused grin. "I know you want to escape now, but that doesn't work for me or the other guests who were in the green mixer and put their trust in me as their host."

I hunched my shoulders and lowered my eyelids. "I'm sorry for going in there. I was just curious..."

"Curious is looking in," he said with a smirk. "You were more than curious."

My face warmed. "Fine. I was more than curious. I didn't mean to upset you or your guest. I didn't recognize anyone, and I won't tell anyone about it."

He shrugged and smiled. "You, like all my guests, signed an ironclad non-disclosure agreement. Your answers in your interview and questionnaire placed you with those that have the same interests. The closed mixer is for those ready to explore those interests. It wasn't for you right now, and you weren't meant to go in there. It is a part of the matchmaking, but for those who want partners that are sexually compatible. What I want to talk to you about is you running away after you participated. As host and part of your experience, I'd like to try to ease some of your concerns."

I stared down at my hands on my lap and sighed. I'd just had the most incredible sexual experience of my life, and it was just a mere blip in his evening. In fact, he was only talking to me as part of his hosting duties, not because he was interested.

"You look upset now," he said, calling me back from my thoughts. "What are you thinking?"

I licked my lips. There was no way I would share how disappointed I was by his response. I was still wounded from being cheated on; the last thing I needed was more rejection. Since he was waiting, I quickly came up with something to say that I thought was safe to ask him about, something Elliott had taunted me with. "What is a tourist?"

"That's not what you were thinking, but I will answer the question." His jaw tightened. "A tourist is a woman or man who wants to experiment with their fantasies and then shun or run away from the reality of their experience."

I scoffed and let my hair fall forward, covering my face. "Sounds like me."

"Pull your hair back so I can see your beautiful face." His words were commanding though his tone was casual.

I smiled and moved my hair back behind my ears. Dane was a charmer, unassuming in his approach. Still, I wanted to explain my behavior lest he get the wrong idea about me. "What happened between us, the three of us...it wasn't like me."

"Is it not like you to regret something? Or for you to let two men make you come?" My cheeks burned hot at his question. I didn't know how to respond. "I didn't say that to embarrass you. We can be open and honest about what happened," he added.

I licked my lips. "All right. Regret, I have plenty of, but the two of you touching me...intimately in a public room isn't me. I'm not usually so..." I paused to search for the right word as to not offend. "Permissive."

What the three of us had done was mind-boggling, crazy, uninhibited, something I didn't imagine happening even in my wildest sexual fantasies, especially with a man like Dane whom, in other circumstances, I'd have a genuine interest in dating. Deep down I knew that was what was really bothering me—Dane's opinion of me.

"I can't imagine what you think."

"What I think of you—is that what you're really asking?" he mused, and he was right. I did want to know.

I sucked in air. "Yes."

He leaned forward, closer to me, and my pulse increased. "I enjoyed watching Elliott touch your pussy when I arrived, and even more when you let both of us make you come. If I had my way, I'd take you in a room with him and we'd fuck you all night." His answer was bold, audacious, and my body clenched in desire in response to everything he mentioned. It had been so long since someone had fucked me. I craved sex, but was this the way to go about it— a night with two strangers? It all seemed incredibly titillating in books, but would I feel even more regret than I already did?

"What are you thinking now?" he asked, interrupting my thoughts.

"I'm thinking how good it must be to have such a carefree life. I would want the person I'm with to care about me, not just get off." My reply was contemptuous, and he sat back in his chair, frowning.

"Who says I—or, for that matter, Elliott, doesn't care? Or that having sex would hold no meaning?" he said. "Personally, I choose those I allow in my bed with care."

I blinked at him. "You say you choose with care, but you're willing to have me as your bed partner with your friend?"

"Yes, I am," he said without hesitation. "We all find each other attractive. You must have answered something on your questionnaire that you have experience or interest, or was it mostly fantasies?"

I nodded.

He smiled. "I would enjoy exploring those with you if I was looking for someone long term, but what I want and expect is much more than what happened between the three of us tonight."

More than what the three of us did together? I wanted to ask more, but a tinge of disappointment blossomed inside of me at his unavailability. I pushed it down. At least he was being up front. After all that had transpired, I wasn't looking for a long-term relationship, nor could I publicly, but even if he were, his interest may go even farther out of my comfort zone. I doubted I'd be able to handle it—though, admittedly, I was thoroughly fascinated by the magnetic man across from me.

I stared down at my hands and gave the only answer I had. "I came here to maybe find the first date I've had in eight years. What I did with you and your friend, I won't shun. I wanted you both to touch me, but I'm not sure I can handle anything more...extreme."

He came over to sit next to me and my heartbeat quickened. He tucked my hair behind my ear and I met his eyes. They were penetrating as he stared into my own. "Your eyes are dark amber. How dark would they turn if I let you come again? How much of a part of those climaxes you have when you masturbate later would you be willing to share? I shouldn't have let you stay there, but I couldn't resist you."

His sexual potency and allure flooded my body with desire again. I didn't know what he meant by what he said, but I was sure spending any more time with him would be my undoing. Before I could say anything, he stood up. Apparently, we had ended our discussion, and there came that twinge of disappointment again as I realized I'd never see him again or even come close to an experience like I'd just had.

"I'll escort you out," Dane said, offering his hand. Once I was on my feet, he took me as far as the limo and secured me inside before speaking again.

"The Agency isn't for you," he said.

I furrowed my brows. "What do you mean?" I wasn't comfortable with the group sex so now he wanted me excluded from all Agency activities?

"I'm not saying this to offend you." His voice softened. "I just think you're not suited for this type of service."

"You don't think I'm suited for matchmaking after I was with you and your friend," I said flatly.

"No, that's not what I meant," he answered then cleared his throat. "I think The Agency is more for people interested in what we did tonight. and as you said, that's not you."

I glanced toward the door. I had, but I wasn't as sure how I felt about it now. "I suppose it's time for me to leave."

"Yes, but Gia," he said. The softness in his voice made me look at him, and he smiled warmly at me. "I'm interested in seeing you again. You are welcome to reach me..." He reached into his pocket and pulled out a card that had his name and a simple sketch of the devil's nymph sculpture. "That is, if you choose to be permissive and want to take me up on my offer."

I put the card in my purse and stared out the window at Dane. He stood in his suit outside the front door, leaving his guests just to attend to me. I couldn't help but wonder what it would be like to remain under his commanding attention for longer than our erotic happenstance.

***

I couldn't stop replaying my encounter with Dane and Elliott when I returned to my place that night. No one outside of my dreams had ever commanded my body like Dane, and it had been the first time in years I didn't have to put aside my own needs or worry about an ego when being brought to orgasm—it was earth-shattering. Just thinking about the precariousness of the orgy caused a thrill to run down my spine and slickness between my thighs. A part of me enjoyed the encounter more because it was dangerous, so much so that I couldn't resist masturbating and reliving the memory, every glide, grasp, and stroke of a hand played out in vivid detail. It was just like Dane had said I would, and I did it over and over again. Yet, I didn't feel satisfied. I wanted to take Dane up on his offer and whatever came with it, though my conscience was telling me I shouldn't.

Still, I couldn't stop thinking about the man. Who was Dane Westbrook?

I had lived most of my life in Seattle and was well versed socially, yet I was perplexed as to why I'd never heard of him. Without my notebooks and records to jog my memory, I drew a blank. Even though he'd mentioned attending one of our many fundraisers, his face and name didn't ring a bell, and from his striking looks, I'd have thought it impossible for him not to leave a lasting impression. My curiosity was enough to get me up from my restless night of sleep and over to my laptop to do a search on him.

The only thing that came up on Google was his design company and some charity work. Even his company profile didn't have a picture or information about his background and only mentioned that he'd studied design at a top art college. I searched more pages of results and still came up with nothing. It was as if he'd appeared out of nowhere. I frowned at the screen as my alarm bells started ringing. A man that went through so much to keep himself private had to be hiding something, right? From working in politics, I learned if you don't piss off someone with more power than you and the press doesn't dig into your life, you could be involved in just about anything.

Then again, he'd hosted a party at his home and had a room full of people there. Those weren't the actions of someone hiding, and I was even more intrigued by him. I wasn't looking for romance and I wanted to have sex, so why not just take Dane up on his offer?

Dane interested and excited me in a way no other man had in a long time. He was incredibly good-looking, confident, secure in himself, and personable. Nonetheless, his closed-off public life and dark private one meant he wouldn't be safe. Then again, I had thought Patrick was safe, and look where that led me.

I couldn't make up my mind on what to do, so instead of returning to bed, I moved on to cleaning up my house, spending hours separating the things I wanted to donate. By afternoon, I had less stuff inside my place.

Unfortunately, it didn't look any better. I needed a remodel, and an excuse to see Dane again.

Before I could talk myself out of it, I went on my computer and sent a message through his company website for a consultation. A tingle went through me at the thought of him seeing my request. It would just be for a remodel, but maybe after a while I could return to The Agency and try another mixer, maybe find a dominant male like Dane.

My stomach sank at the thought of searching for a match. I didn't know if I would have the same visceral reaction to another man, and when it came to submission, I only knew what I read in romance books. This was real life. How would I be able to communicate what I really wanted if I didn't know myself? While I wasn't interested in complete control, the way Dane had orchestrated everything that happened to me had left me admitting a more than casual interest. For the time being, I wanted someone who would at least teach me the basics.

Still on my laptop, I typed *D/s* into the search engine and was instantly overwhelmed by all the websites.

Online wasn't exactly secret, but you didn't have to disclose your identity unless you were ready to meet someone. After browsing a few websites, I chose *Changing Fates* and created a profile name adding my old college dorm room number to the end, *CuriousG192*, and logged in. It had online stories, a glossary of terms, and a code of practice: safe, sane, and consensual. It was nothing I hadn't read in a few books, but this time, it was real. There were pages of images of couples in bondage gear, ranging from a woman sitting with her hands behind her back and her head lowered to full-on leather and chains tied to St. Andrew's crosses. I was fascinated, but so far, nothing connected to what I had experienced the night before. I was about to leave the website when a flashing red light lit up the corner of my screen. Clicking it with my mouse, I found it was someone trying to contact me in a chat room. A thrill went down my spine, and I smiled. *Why not?* Maybe there could be someone on the website that could point me in the direction of where I could start. I opened the private window and up came the message with the contact and his screen name, Master T. I opened the window and read his message.

Master. T: Get on your knees

I furrowed my brows. Was this a joke or a test of some kind? I didn't understand. I typed back.

CuriousG192: Why would I do that and how would you know I'm doing it if we can't see each other?

Master. T: I said, get on your knees you filthy slut

I pursed my lips. He was calling me names and wanting me to take orders? Was this how you found a dominant male to play with?

CuriousG192: Are you serious? I just logged on. Can we just talk?

Master. T: Poser bitch!

My face burned and I closed the window. Uneasiness mingled with my embarrassment at my lack of experience. I was sure there could be nice people on the website from some of the profiles, but this wasn't working for me. I now appreciated all the preliminary screening The Agency had done. Was my only option to return to The Agency and Dane?

Dane was the only one I was genuinely interested in getting to know at The Agency, and he had offered to see me again.

I wasn't sure about having casual sex with Dane, but I had made my mind up about the website. I went to my account settings and scrolled down to the bottom of the page.

You have selected to delete your account. Are you sure? There is no going back and you will have to resubmit your profile to regain your membership.

I clicked the *Yes* button and stared at the goodbye screen. Even after that disappointing exchange, I was still left wanting, but I wasn't ready to go. I'd find another way to start.

CHAPTER FIVE

Astrid: Merry Christmas. Hope you enjoyed yours, though I wish you'd have come over.

Gia: Thanks. I slept in and opened presents. Thanks for the new robe.

Astrid: You picked it out lol and you are a liar. You worked!

Gia: A little.

I laughed out loud. She was right. I had logged into my work email and cleared most of my inbox. I'd also gotten a jump on some of the new marketing and advertising proposals. I wasn't complaining. I loved every minute of it.

Astrid: I just wish you'd take some time to rest and enjoy yourself. BTW, how did the mixer go?

Gia: It didn't go great.

Astrid: Oh, come on Gia. You must have met someone.

I bit my lip. What could I share? The Agency hadn't said I couldn't speak about it, but while I wasn't exactly feeling bad about what I'd done, I didn't want to share with her about the orgy or what I had done.

Gia: I did meet a couple of guys, but I don't think we connected.

Astrid: You didn't find your match at this one, but it was only your first. Don't give up. Go to another one.

I blew out a breath. *No thanks.* The thought of going back to another mixer wasn't something I was sure about. I hadn't wanted to bother Liz until after the holiday, but when I tried after Christmas, I wasn't able to reach her. I also had no response to my query for the remodel; my brief encounter with Dane Westbrook was over. I wasn't sure if I wanted to try a matchmaking service again. In the meantime, I'd had enough of staying inside my house so I decided to go to the gym, and I told Astrid as much.

Astrid: Wear something cute. Who knows who you might meet there.

I smiled and put my phone away. I hadn't thought of looking cute, but I had put on a new pink and gray track suit. I wasn't a regular at the gym lately and had to search for my pass. Since it was Christmas vacation for a lot of people, I thought it would be less busy, but it wasn't. Begrudgingly, I snatched up a couple of too-heavy free weights to perform a toning routine I remembered from years past. I was on my third rep when a pair of turquoise athletic shoes crossed my line of vision. A glance up revealed they belonged to Liz, who was dressed in a gray track suit that was zipped up under her chin and looked out of place in the humid atmosphere of the gym. I looked at her face and did a triple take. She was pale with a red tinge around her eyes, a far cry from the Liz I had seen a few weeks before.

"What's wrong?" I asked after we greeted each other.

Her eyes darted away from me. "Holiday blues. I might be coming down with something too. Sorry I haven't been in touch after your night out."

I lowered my brows. It was clear as rain that there was more to it. I decided to try another approach. "It's completely understandable. You were on vacation just like me. How about we share a smoothie now, if you have some time?"

She hesitated but then agreed, though when we were in line to place orders at the juice bar, she refused everything but water. When we were comfortably seated, Liz turned and looked at me, but I couldn't quite read her expression. "How did the mixer go?"

I lifted a shoulder. "I met a few people, but I don't think it's for me."

More time away from the event and the fact that no one at Dane's company had replied to my remodel inquiry had led me to see it in a different light.

She sighed heavily. "Good. You don't need to go there again. There are plenty of other places to meet eligible men."

"That's quite the change in attitude since you signed me up," I joked, swatting her arm playfully. She winced, and I raised my brows. "Are you in pain?"

She wouldn't meet my eyes. "It's just the strain from exercise. I'll be fine. I'm glad I ran into you. I'm sorry I was so pushy about going to The Agency. I shouldn't have done that. I wasn't thinking. I was acting like a stupid school girl."

"You weren't," I said, frowning. "You're being way too hard on yourself. It wasn't all bad. I met Dane." I couldn't hide the smile or the heat that rushed to my face. "He was charming, but he was busy hosting."

She gave me a smile that didn't quite reach her eyes. "Dane's in a relationship—"

"He's in a relationship?" I repeated incredulously.

Dane had offered me a threesome with his friend, but he was in a relationship? Maybe the relationship was open? Whatever he was doing was a tangled mess I didn't want to get involved in. I glanced over at Liz, and it seemed she was miles away.

"Yes," she affirmed. "At least that's what Sir—"

"Sir? Why are you calling him that—are you two role-playing?"

Her eyes darted away from me. "Yeah, that's what we were doing...role-playing. Sorry to confuse you."

"You didn't need to explain. I was just curious," I replied slowly. "Anyway, I did meet someone else, a man named Elliott—"

"Elliott Carmichael?" she said with a twist to her mouth.

"I don't know his last name," I replied. I did remember the lustful way he'd stared at me from the floor when he stroked me to climax. I lowered my head as heat returned to my face.

"I can see from your expression, he's one and the same," she said in a clipped tone. "Trust me, he's bad news. Stay away from him."

My stomach knotted. *Too late.* "What do you mean? He seemed nice..." Well, he had been when he touched me.

She grimaced. "He's not."

"What do you know about him?" I pressed.

She rubbed her neck. "He leaves a string of women wanting in his wake. He's not serious about anyone. He's just after sex."

"What's wrong with that?" I said, laughing a little, but Liz didn't join in. "I thought sex was what you were encouraging me to do just a few days ago when you mentioned The Agency."

"I was...I am, but not with guys like Elliott who are *only* after sex," she said. "You're only just divorced. You wouldn't want to get mixed up in anything too risky," she added.

"Like the green mixer?" I whispered.

Her eyes widened and shifted around. "I'm surprised you were allowed in one of them." Her expression changed to concern. "Or did something happen to you?"

"No...I sort of stumbled upon it," I responded.

Her face pinched. "You didn't participate?" she asked cautiously.

I licked my lips. "No."

It wasn't a complete lie, I told myself. *Shit, it is. Now I sound like Patrick.* Even so, my brief time at the orgy wasn't something I'd share with anyone anyway.

"Good." Her shoulders dropped. "If I'd know there would be one at your mixer, I'd never have sent you there. Did someone pressure you to go in? Did Dane—"

"He didn't," I said, but now I was curious. "Why do you ask? Do you know something about Dane hurting someone?"

"No," she answered. "I just don't think going to those types of parties is a good idea. I don't want you pressured into doing anything you don't want to do."

"Okay," I said. "But I was assured by Dane that everyone...in the room was there by their own choice. I don't know...it wasn't for me, but it didn't seem bad."

She lowered her eyelids. "Probably from the outside, it wouldn't look too bad. I'm not against experimenting, and at first, the multiple partners feel good, but then afterward, if you can't handle it, it leaves you feeling empty. Expectations change...but once you open those doors with a partner, you can't close them." She ran her hand over her arm in a way that had me thinking she had more knowledge of the subject than she was willing to tell me then and there.

"Is that what happened to you?" I asked.

"No. It's hard to explain," she replied cryptically then went quiet as I waited for her to elaborate. She moved the sleeve of her jacket, and I saw a black leather ribbon at her wrist that had a small lock on it.

"What's that?" I reached out to examine it closer, but she quickly pulled her sleeve back down. "It's nothing."

My lips pursed. "But you're covering it," I pointed out, my voice lowering. "Did he hurt you?"

"No," she said firmly. "It's just a little tight," she said, waving her hand dismissively when I tried to touch it.

My brows puckered at the way it dug into her skin. Surely she could get rid of it. "Take it off—or did you lose the key? You can get a locksmith or a jeweler to take it off. There's one not far from here.

"No." She pulled her arm away and fixed her jacket down over the wristband. "It's...not bothering me."

"You're lying—you look uncomfortable," I protested.

She jutted her chin out. "It's...it's my business." She would have been more convincing if she hadn't stammered.

"Oh, come on Liz. I'm not here to judge, just to listen," I prodded. It was too much of a change in her behavior for me to just ignore it. "Something's going on. You can tell me anything."

She sighed heavily. "I'll just say, I pushed for something I wasn't ready for, and it won't happen again. I also realized I pushed you to try something you weren't ready for, so I'm glad you're finished with The Agency. Promise me you're done with them?" She seemed so upset that I sought to assure her, though I had already made up my mind.

"I have no plans to go there again," I told her. Truly, she didn't need to keep warning me. I didn't plan to see Elliott or go to any mixers again. Dane had been pretty clear that he didn't think I was suited for The Agency, and I doubted I'd even be invited again if I tried. The topic seemed to distress Liz, so I decided to change the subject. "Things are better for you now," I pointed out. "You have Marco."

"Do I, or does he have me?" Her voice broke miserably. She looked at her watch. "I need to get going."

Before I could say anything else, my cell phone buzzed.

She motioned for me to take the call and quickly left before I could say anything more. I was worried about her and made a mental note to call her as I absently answered the call.

"Hello Gia, it's Dane. You contacted my company for a remodel."

I couldn't stop the flutter in my chest at the sound of the deep tenor of his voice. "I'm at the gym, one second." I swiftly moved to stand in the hallway leading to the swimming pool for more privacy and cleared my throat before returning to the line. "Yes. My place needs a remodel. You had mentioned the possibility at the party."

"I did, but that was before we had an intimate moment," he said quietly. I found his choice of words gratifying, but then he added, "*If* the remodel is the reason you contacted me, be sure about it, because I never mix work with sex."

I pressed my lips together. *You just mix in extra partners to spice things up.* I shook my head, reminding myself that it was none of my business, though I couldn't resist asking, "Do women often call you for sex?"

"Why do you care about other women?" he said without missing a beat, answering my question with another. His voice sounded amused.

"I don't, I was just curious," I said as I glanced around. "If, say, I was interested in sex, what would you do?"

"I'd cut the meeting I'm in short and come over right now."

My nerves were jumping as my mind imagined what it might be like for a man I barely knew to come over to have sex with me. Hell, I never had one-night stands. The four men total I had dated, including Patrick, had waited months before we had sex. "It's that easy for you?" I asked, slightly flabbergasted.

"It's easy for me to decide to have sex with you right now. Sex is where things start with me."

"What about your partner?" I asked. "Wouldn't she be upset at you dropping everything to come have sex with me?" I held my breath.

"What are you talking about?" he asked.

I stubbed my shoe into the tile floor. "I heard you're already in a relationship, though you didn't mention it at the party. Perhaps it's okay with her, but personally I don't like to get mixed up in romantic entanglements." The line went quiet, and I anxiously waited for him to deny what Liz had told me.

"I see," he said. "I don't share my private life with those I'm not intimate with. You're conflicted, and I understand. I will say monogamy isn't where I start. It moves too fast into attachments without even knowing if you're well-matched for sex."

I wanted to argue against it, but what he said made sense. I had no doubt now that Patrick and I were intimately incompatible now. Still, I was conflicted about wanting to know more and frustrated by his unwillingness to share with me.

Before I could say anything else, he said, "What I offer is too much for you right now and that's fine. We'll stick to business. I'll send someone over for a consultation. We could fit you in today, how does that sound?"

"Sure. That would be great," I replied dully.

Once again, disappointment washed over me. He asked a few more questions about my house before ending the call. Professionally, I was impressed with the work I saw on the website and in his home, and there was no harm in agreeing to a preliminary assessment of the property. It wasn't a commitment to work with him, so it was fine...or so I told myself.

I was attracted and frustrated at the same time. Dane had seemed so up front at the party, but the second I questioned his personal life, he shut me down—except for sex, which he was clear was going to be on his terms. I thought perhaps I should take Liz's advice about him. She wasn't herself after getting mixed up with people in his company, but even after I went back to finishing up my workout routine and took a shower at the gym before heading home, I couldn't stop thinking about him.

CHAPTER SIX

When I went to pull into my driveway upon returning home, I was surprised to find a silver Mercedes parked out front. The car had left me enough space to drive around to park in the garage. Once I stopped in my usual spot, I got out, went back to the driveway, and pressed the button for the electronic door to come down.

"Miss me?" purred a deep voice behind me.

My face heated. It wasn't Dane; he'd said he didn't mix business with pleasure, but apparently he hadn't told Elliott, whom I now faced. His brilliant, crystal blue eyes bore into mine with a knowing that immediately set me on edge. They brought me right back to him on his knees before me with his fingers bringing me to a climax.

If the flashback wasn't enough, I was overcome with lust. He looked too damn good in his structured indigo blazer and dark jeans. They were tailored to fit what I had little doubt was a well-toned body underneath. *Shit*. Now I was imagining him naked. I inhaled a heavenly scent of expensive cologne that was just another lure into the Elliott zone, one that was too much right then, especially with Liz's warning against him. "No, I haven't given you much thought since the mixer."

Elliott's mouth turned up in a smile. "You're lying. I can take just about anything but liars. I was there—I know better."

My cheeks burned. Was I that transparent?

He leaned close to me. "If you want me to stroke your pussy again, Gia, I'll let Dane know, since you're interested in him. I'll ask him not to make you beg before you come, but I can't promise you that."

My brain didn't intend for any of it to happen. My body, on the other hand, was pulsing at just the thought. Still, his assumption that Dane would dictate what I did or didn't do bothered me. We had agreed to only do business, and that was how this meeting was going to go.

I squared my shoulders. "I contacted Westbrook Designs for a consultation for remodeling my home. I didn't realize he would send you."

"I handle initial consultations for clients planning a complete remodel," he replied. "I admit I flirted, but WB Designs can do your job. If you need to see samples of our work, I have our portfolio in my car. Our most recent designs were featured in the November issue of *Architectural Digest*. If you don't think you can work with me, I can call Dane to send someone else over?"

I crossed my arms. To be honest, I was uncomfortable. "I was caught off guard by you being here, but I'd still like to continue with the *consultation.*" I stressed the last word to make it clear I may or may not use Dane and Elliott's company.

We walked a few paces and he frowned. "Your hair is dripping down the back of your jacket—do you realize it's below freezing out today?"

"I went to the gym and now I'm going from the car inside. It's hardly anything to worry about," I tried to explain, but oddly my excuse still concerned him.

"That's what people think, and then they get sick," he argued. "Get inside and dry your hair now, and I'll do the walkthrough of your place."

I was both surprised and annoyed by his orders, but strangely I walked with him with plans to do just as he asked. We were about to go inside when I heard the sound of a car door closing. I looked down the driveway and saw Liz. Inwardly, I cringed at the twist of her mouth as her gaze shifted between the two of us.

Elliott smirked. "Well that explains your less than warm greeting," he said to me. "Hello Liz—"

"It's Ms. Crenshaw to you," Liz interjected, her tone curt as she corrected him.

Great. I'd figured she disliked him, but I hadn't realized the extent. They had some sort of history, and I thought it would be better to stop them now before any more conflict arose between the two of them.

"Elliott is here to look at the place. You left before I had the chance to tell you about the consultation for a remodel. I didn't expect you to stop by," I babbled.

Liz relaxed some. "I know. I was wondering if I could borrow your shawl for an event I'm going to in San Francisco tomorrow."

I smiled. "Of course. I just have to find it." I motioned for them to follow me up the steps, despite the tension.

Once inside, Elliott wrinkled his nose as he circled the living room. "I feel like we've taken a time machine to the seventies, and not in a good way. Did the furniture come with it?"

"No, smarty-pants," I said, trying hard to suppress my smile. He wasn't far off in his criticism. The place looked like a dump. I'd chosen this house because the asking price was well below market, it was in a great neighborhood, and it was available to move into quickly. In hindsight, it was impulsive and unwise. As a single woman, this large house didn't suit me at all, nor did the green and brown multicolored shag carpet or the faded gold and plaid paisley wallpaper that clashed with the knotted cherry wood and stucco paneling. Perhaps the previous owner hadn't been able to decide what they wanted to do.

"If you need me to stay with you, Gia," Liz said, glaring at Elliott, "I don't need to be anywhere for the next couple of hours."

"I could come back, or do you have the hours after that free too, Liz?" he mused, smiling over at her. Liz wasn't laughing or moving from her spot.

"Thanks for the offer, but I do need a remodel, and having their expertise in design isn't something I'd like to pass up," I explained. "I'll go get your shawl. I'll just be a minute."

She folded her arms. "All right. I'll wait for you here."

I kicked off my shoes then took the stairs two at a time and threw things around in my closet to find the shawl Liz wanted to borrow. I was in a rush to separate them. However, the sound of their raised voices on my way back to where they waited for me had me slowing down to listen to what they were arguing about.

"It was a mistake sending Gia to The Agency," she said. "She doesn't need to get mixed up in this. She's not going back. If you and Dane had any decency, you'd turn down this job."

"Oh, clutch the pearls, we must be decent," Elliott said mockingly. "Nothing will happen that she doesn't want to—"

"We know that's not true," she snapped.

"It is with me," Elliott said sharply. "You're crying foul now after everything—"

"I'm not," she said heatedly. "And please be quiet. You don't know me or what you're talking about."

"I know that you like to upgrade," he said scornfully.

"It wasn't like that," she muffled.

"Seriously, what do you want?" His tone was gentle.

"Like you'd help me now, even if I told you," she grumbled. "Just stay away from me and my friends."

No more hanging back. I hurried down the rest of the stairs noisily and just like I suspected, they stopped arguing. I went to Liz.

"I found it." I held out the shawl and she took it. "We'll talk later, okay?"

She glowered at Elliott. "Oh, we will, most definitely."

I gave her a hug at the door and watched her drive off. I came back in to find that Elliott had moved on to my kitchen. He was jotting down notes on a notepad. "This room will need to be gutted. Hope you like takeout." He winked at me.

I crossed my arms. "Actually, I'm no longer sure about the remodel, at least not with Dane's company."

He came over and stood in front of me. "That's fine—even better, actually. We both know that's not why you called in the first place. You wanted to take Dane up on his offer to have sex with us."

I looked away, my face hot. I couldn't deny it—I had considered Dane's offer—but I offered some further explanation. "At the time I sent the message, things were different. I was curious, and you were pretty clear from that night that you considered me a tourist."

"You were one," he said, not backing down. "You enjoyed us both playing with your pussy, but afterward you tried to make us feel like shit for doing it to you."

I lifted my chin, despite the heat growing in my face at his crass words. "No, that's not all that happened. I admit that I wanted to and agreed to allow you both to...do that to me. I just had never done that before and I was embarrassed, but I have since found out that Dane's involved with someone."

Elliott sighed. "It's complicated, but you're not looking for a relationship, are you?"

"No," I admitted. "But I hate cheaters. Even if he was in an open relationship or whatever, someone is bound to get hurt."

"No one will," he said. "Dane has his interests, like having me in the mix, but you know that already."

"Yes," I said. "But is there anything else?" I was curious.

"That's for you to find out if you decide to take Dane up on his offer," he replied. "What I will share is this: if it ever turned personal, he wouldn't change his kinks. If you already feel like it's too much for you, you should walk away like your friend wants you to do."

I glared over at him. "Did something happen between you and Liz?"

"Nothing happened with *me*," he said, rubbing his jaw. "She thinks she knows something about me, but she's judging me by whatever gossip she heard."

I shrugged. I believed there was more to it, but neither one of them was willing to share. I also thought it better to not jump to conclusions.

"Fair enough, but still, she's really unhappy about something."

"Sometimes people get caught up," he said with a sigh. "But let's get back to you, me, and Dane—what's keeping you from taking him up on his offer?"

I rubbed my arms. "I don't know."

"That's not a no," he replied with another wink.

I tried to hold in my smile. It wasn't.

"Now that we're okay"—he tugged my hair until it fell from my bun—"go dry your hair and put on a dress." There went his hand, this time with a cup and a squeeze on my buttocks. "Sexy."

I pushed his hand aside, but I couldn't hide my grin. "Stop flirting."

He was infuriating, but I liked being called sexy.

"Show me the rest of your house and we'll dry your hair." He placed his hand on my lower back and we moved through a quick tour that ended in my bedroom, where I went into the bathroom to dry my hair. He came in after a few minutes and took over brushing it. I thought it odd that he was surprisingly gentle.

"You do this often?" I mused.

"I did for my mother before she died," he said. "She had pancreatitis and many aliments growing up. My sister and I did what we could. It took some moments away from her pain."

My heart turned over, watching him try to school his face. I knew that pain; I had it too. "My mom died from an aneurism before I left for college. It came as a shock. My father remarried. He's in Palm Springs."

"We have that in common too, but it's Florida for my dad, and his third wife. We'll leave it at that." The amusement that surrounded him left, and I gave him a side hug. "I'm all right," he said then let me go and followed me back into the bedroom. We walked into my closet. "Business suits and more business suits," he mused.

"I've been meaning to shop for new clothing." I grimaced at my selection. "Most of what I have in the closet is for work or political fundraisers." For a few minutes we went through the racks of clothing in silence. He broke it first.

"You know, Gia..." he said in a low tone.

I paused between the racks and looked at him. "Yes?"

"I'm all right with you being curious about having sex with the two of us," he said. "I can also promise you that when we all do, it'll be the best sex of your life."

I lowered my brows. "The best sex of my life? I can't imagine sex being that good." Moving some clothes on the top shelf dislodged a couple of boxes, which Elliott quickly set back in place for me. The collar on his shirt came untucked at the neck, and I reached over to fix it.

His face softened. "It would be, and then some. Dane would spoil you if you'd let him, beautiful." His fingers traced the side of my face and down my neck, making me shiver.

Just Dane? I shook my head. What was I thinking?

That was when I realized my hand had moved down from his collar to the front of his shirt, and I was feeling the ridges of his muscles rippling underneath.

My eyes slid back to his and our gazes locked together. All the air left the room. It was like slow motion watching his head come closer. I could have moved away, but I didn't, and when his lips met mine, mine parted.

Elliott groaned approvingly as he glided his tongue in and slid it seductively with an eagerness and demanding I had never experienced before. I found myself responding in kind, my tongue intertwining with his.

AMÉLIE S. DUNCAN

It would have been perfect to put my arms around him. Though it felt good, it also felt off. I was genuinely interested in having sex with Dane, but there I was again making out with someone who was not only his friend, but his business partner too.

I broke away and sucked in air, my confusion overtaking the enjoyment of the moment.

"Dane is fine with you kissing me," he reassured. "It's good with us. We've shared women before."

My brows furrowed. "Maybe, but I'm not sure if I'm fine with it. I don't know what's gotten into me."

He sighed and took out his phone. "You're doing what you want and not worrying about it. It's freeing. If you want Dane's take on it, I'll get him to tell you."

I tugged his arm. "No. I don't want to interrupt whatever he's doing." Interrupting was one of Patrick's pet peeves, which made it ironic that he always expected me to drop

142

everything for him. I shook my head and tried to move all thoughts of Patrick to the back of my mind.

"Dane will make time to speak to you," he assured me. I watched him, not knowing what to make of it, or of myself.

My conflicted mind had me pulling into myself by wrapping my arms around my body. I was certain I wanted to spend more time with Dane, but I was also attracted to Elliott. I didn't know how it would work.

Elliott talked to him then held out his phone for me to take.

I took a deep breath and answered. "Hi Dane."

"Hello, Gia," he said, and I couldn't stop the thrill that ran up my spine at hearing him say my name. "Elliott said you stopped a kiss because you were worried about what I'd think. I'm feeling encouraged—that's what you're having a hard time understanding. I know you're attracted to him. You want him too, don't you?" There was no mistaking the delight in his voice.

"I...I don't know," I stammered.

"Just say how you feel," he said encouragingly.

"I considered taking you up on your offer of...sex," I admitted, my face burning. "But I don't know if I can have sex with..." My voice wavered. I couldn't bring myself to say *with Elliott too* with him right there staring at me. Fortunately, Dane understood.

"You're attracted to Elliott," he said.

"Yes, but I was hoping maybe the two of us could talk more, maybe go slower than how things went at the mixer."

"I don't do that. If there is no attraction, no passion, I don't waste my time with dinner and conversation," he replied bluntly. "My idea of going slow starts with sex, and I'm turned on by what is happening with you and Elliot right now."

"Is that how things worked with you and your partner?" I said, broaching the subject again. "I don't want to hurt her."

He went quiet for a few moments and then answered. "She's not with me, but that's about as much as I wish to discuss on the matter."

I frowned and took a few steps away then leaned against one of the built-in shelves, ever aware that Elliott was near and watching me. I didn't exactly understand what he meant. She wasn't with him, but were they still together? Why wasn't I willing to walk away knowing he had someone else, even if she was okay with sharing him? Everything about the situation was compromising the person I thought I was. Never would I have ever imagined myself being involved with a man who belonged to another woman. Then again, he had said she wasn't with him anymore.

I felt so exposed in that moment. Elliott's kiss had left me wanting more, and I was slick between my thighs at the prospect. Why should it matter so much if it was only going to be one night with him, or with them both?

My whole body burned with anticipation. I eyed Elliott, who stood quietly staring over at me while Dane and I spoke. Starting with someone other than the person I was most interested in seemed wrong. "Maybe Elliott and I can try another kiss?"

"If you can come from that kiss, you can try," he replied dryly. "I know you can from his touch, and we both know that's not what you really want. Elliott touching you isn't a deal-breaker for me. I want Elliott to make you come, and I want to listen to it happen. You want it too. Now, hand back the phone to Elliott." His tone held an authority; something about it freed me of my reservations and heated my body with liquid fire. In the end, it was all me, and he was right—I not only wanted Elliott to touch me, it turned me on to think Dane would be listening in while he did it.

Elliott took his phone from my trembling hand and placed it on a shelf facing upward, letting me know they must have discussed this possibility and were already in agreement. His blue eyes were dark and hot as his gaze swept over me

Waves of heat surged through me and I squeezed my thighs together to soothe the ache, my hand moving along the button of my pants. "Elliott," I moaned. I didn't know what to do or how to start.

He was quick to grab my hips. "Touching yourself will earn you a spanking when we're having sex together, unless I command you to do it, but you didn't know that yet. Now, kiss me."

He took my head in his hands. His fingers twisted in my hair, tilting my head up toward his own, and then his open lips came down on mine with a ferocity that took my breath away. I felt the powerful press of his lips as he stroked his mouth against my own. If I'd had doubts about what Elliott wanted or thought of me, they were gone. My need and desire awakened as I let loose some of my own control. I gave in to his kisses, which had a faint taste of cinnamon, his tongue warm and soft. It felt so good I could have continued to kiss him all night, but then he broke the kiss, pulled my jeans down to my knees, and cupped me between my legs.

A rush of excitement went through me at his command. My body came to life and my shyness ebbed as I worked my jeans and underwear down to my ankles. I was tapping into that sexual part of me again, that throbbing need Elliott seemed to recognize as a part of me.

My eyes flicked to Elliott, who was still staring hard at me, though his gaze was now lower. He ran his tongue over his lips suggestively and my body tightened. The air thickened between us, and for a few seconds all we could hear was the sound of our breaths as I worked up the nerve to place his hand where he wanted me to, where I wanted him to be. It was just so brash.

"Elliott," I whispered. "I don't know..."

"All you need to think about is how much I want to feel you come again," he said.

Why not do what I wanted? This was for me.

He took my hand, placed it between his legs, and moved it against the erection filling his jeans. Feeling Elliott so turned on sent heat surging to my already aching, throbbing clit and was the catalyst that moved me to take Elliott's large hand between my thighs. My skin tingled and I gasped at the first contact of his fingers as he touched the smooth surface of my mound. A delicious shiver of want went through me as he placed two fingers around my clit, stroking down through my slick folds. I moaned and moved against his touch.

"She's killing me." He said it loud enough that I was sure Dane could hear.

Dane's voice came through the phone. "Bring the phone close so I can hear the sound of you stroking her wet pussy."

Elliott picked up the phone with his free hand then brought it down close to my body, and we both moaned as I gapped my legs wider and he strummed his fingers through my wetness. I was too far gone to think. All I wanted to do was come. "You've got a pretty little pussy. You're going to squeeze the fuck out of our cocks." Elliott's voice was harsh in my ear as he put down the phone. He pushed two fingers inside me. "Let Dane hear you."

My moans were loud between my shallow breaths as Elliott continued to fuck me with his fingers.

Elliott worked in a third finger. "Show me how you'll move when I fuck you." Grasping tight to his shoulders, I let out a cry.

"Damn, put her on live so I can watch her do it," Dane commanded.

Elliott pressed the app on his phone and held the screen down as I moved my hips against his fingers. Knowing Dane was watching now made my walls tighten. Elliott let go of the phone, and I was too gone to stop. I went with it, losing myself in the exquisite sensation. Elliott's fingers moved in and out of me faster, his thumb pressing down on my clit until I stiffened in his arms as I came. This time I didn't fall under the weight of self-condemnation; I quietly relaxed my face into his shoulder. I felt light as the climactic bliss coursed through my body.

He held me close and kept stroking inside of me as I rode out the sensations. "You're sexy when you come, Gia. Fuck, take out my cock and squeeze it."

I feverishly obeyed his request, fumbling with the button of his pants and reaching into his boxers to fulfill his demand. I took his engorged hot shaft in my hand, wrapping around his thick girth and squeezing.

"Open your legs." He stroked a hand between my legs then used my essence as a glide before fisting his cock, my hands moving down to caress his balls. My eyes were fixed on the powerful, fast strokes as he worked his hard length.

Elliott inhaled sharply. "That's right, Gia. Fuck...just like that."

My strokes matched his eagerness, our breaths erratic. I wanted nothing else but to see him come.

"Get down and open your shirt," he said. "I'm coming on your tits."

I quickly did as he asked, opening my shirt and taking my bra off, and his release came just as frenzied as mine had. He let out a yell as he detonated, his cum flowing hot over my breasts.

Our eyes met, and I shuddered at the intensity in his gaze.

He broke first. "Let's clean up and I'll get Dane back on the line." He spoke briefly to Dane, then followed me. We had just stepped through the door of the bedroom when Elliott clasped my body, crushing it against his. He yanked my hair back and wrapped it around his hand, his mouth coming down hard on mine. His possession was dizzying, addictive. I couldn't get enough. Just as quickly as he'd taken me, he let me go. "Dane's waiting. You need to talk to him," he got out between breaths.

I sucked in air. *Yes, Dane.* Elliott withdrew from me and we quietly cleaned up then returned to the closet to collect his phone. While my mind raced with all that had happened, I didn't feel much regret like I had at the mixer. I admitted to myself that I wanted this.

"You'll take care of me later," Dane said to me when we reached him again by phone. His voice was coarse, his breathing hard, his control just as shattered as my own. Without a doubt, he meant sex with him. His invitation was a passionate challenge, and with it came a throbbing need that rose within me at the prospect. Deep down, I knew such a consuming attraction to a man could be perilous to my emotions, but I couldn't bring myself to run away. I could refuse, but I felt my resolve waning. I was still willing, regardless of how little I knew about them.

"Yes, I will, Dane."

CHAPTER SEVEN

I lay down on my bed after Elliott left, thinking about Dane. We'd agreed to have me come over after six. I was sure now that it wasn't just my long dry spell that had me doing things I wouldn't normally have done before. Something about the way the two of them guided me, the way Dane took control...it got to me. It was under his direction and control that Elliott had touched me again, and the sinfulness of him listening in and watching had intensified the orgasm to combustion. I was captivated, even though I barely knew Dane. The little I did know showed he operated well beyond my experience sexually. Nevertheless, I couldn't suppress the growing excitement within at what sex would be like between us. I had little doubt I'd find it satisfying, but would he with me?

A man connected to a mysterious matchmaking service who hosted orgies in his home must have seen and done more than I could ever imagine. If that wasn't enough to worry about, there was the possibility that he was still involved with someone. He had said the woman he was with was gone, but did gone mean forever?

Evidently, he wasn't willing to share more than his body, but did I need to know everything if we weren't going to date? I couldn't anyway right now, so did it matter? Maybe I was making excuses because I wanted him for a fling, not just a one-night stand. After some more cleaning and a short nap, I awoke with the same worrying thoughts and even considered calling off my plans with Dane. My thoughts were interrupted by the buzzing of an incoming text. It was Liz, and my stomach instantly sank. I had completely forgotten about her.

Liz: I'm worried about you. Did Elliott leave?

I was perplexed by her message. In all the time I'd known Liz, she'd never behaved like a nagging mom, so I didn't understand why she was being so pushy about Elliott. Was she into Elliott herself? I would ask them both about it later, but for now I tried to ease her mind and wrote back.

Gia: He did. Stop worrying. Everything is fine. What about you?

Liz: It's too late for me.

I rubbed my neck to pat down the hairs that had risen there. She wasn't one for dramatics either, but new relationships could take you on a bit of a rollercoaster ride. Still, her message unnerved me.

Gia: What do you mean? You're kind of freaking me out over here. Did you and Marco break up?

I pressed send, but I was also considering calling her to talk.

Liz: Sorry about that last message. Let's have lunch when I return from San Francisco.

I called her anyway, but she didn't pick up. I thought perhaps time away was what she needed. I called Astrid to see what she thought of Liz's odd message, and to calm my nerves. Once Astrid got past me not sharing with her about seeing Liz with her boyfriend, she was ready to offer her advice.

"Liz sounds a bit dramatic, but new relationships can be like that. Liz is smart. If she wants to move on, she will, but when she's ready."

I chewed on my lip. "That was what I thought too. I'll just ask her to meet up when she gets back from her trip."

"Me too," Astrid said. "I don't like being left out of the loop. Since I have you on the phone, would you like to come over and hang out? I can get Tim to watch Jacob. We're not leaving to go to his parents' until tomorrow night."

"I can't tonight. I have plans," I said in as casual a tone as I could muster.

"Oh, you do. With who?" she asked, and I smiled at the delight in her tone.

"It's someone from the mixer, but it's not a date or anything big," I replied. *Except we are planning to have sex.* I decided to keep that part to myself.

"Why are you being mysterious? You can tell me something, at least who it is," she prodded.

"It's Dane, the host of the mixer," I told her. "But before you get excited, it's nothing serious. He's not really...interested in dating. We're just staying in at his place."

"Ohhh," she said, slowly getting what I meant without me having to spell out that we were just getting together for sex. "Well, good for you. I hope the sex is good."

"Me too," I said as I touched my warm cheeks. "I better go get ready."

"Have fun," she said, and we laughed. "Seriously, you do whatever feels right for you."

"Thank you," I said then hung up. It was good to share some of what was going on with Astrid, but I didn't want to share everything since I didn't really know much about it myself.

I went and changed into a nice black lace bra and underwear set. I dressed in a black crepe wraparound dress with thigh-highs and heeled boots. It was suitable for a night out, though Dane hadn't made plans other than sex. Even so, I quickly put on my coat and left the house, not lingering, lest my nerves get the better of me.

***

Dane answered the door when I rang the doorbell. Somehow, I managed to keep my cool, though his silvery gaze burned into me with such a dauntless, salacious scrutiny. I was sure he had me naked in his mind already. He wet his lips then curved them up into a bright smile that shined through the dusting of stubble on his jaw. His appeal was devastating, and a deep shudder coursed through me at knowing I'd soon know him carnally. My thoughts heightened my nerves, and I trembled. Dane closed the distance between us as he placed his arms firmly around my waist.

"Try to relax for me. Nothing will harm you, I promise," he whispered soothingly. He didn't break our connection right away, and I remained in his arms as he rubbed my back, enjoying the way he held me close. His arms were warm and comforting, and I found the tension in my body start to release, though my pulse remained erratic in anticipation of what would come next between us.

I took a deep breath in, and with it came the tantalizing scent of his aftershave. Everything about this man was seductive.

"We'll start in one of my guest bedrooms," he announced once we reached the top of the stairs. Anticipation took over my nervousness as Dane took my hand, leading me forward.

We would be following his rules and going straight to bed, and in all honestly, I didn't want to wait. I wanted him immediately.

Dane turned on the lights and revealed a bedroom that was larger and better furnished than my own, but all I could think about was the hard pound of my heartbeat as Dane brought us over to the king-sized bed. It bounced us closer when we sat down on the edge of it together. Dane gripped my side to steady me, and I shuddered at his touch. My eyes lifted, and I couldn't tear my gaze away from his. He was positively mesmerizing.

His large hands cupped my face. I shivered as his tongue slipped inside my parted lips. The caress of his mouth was searing, demanding. It was an exquisite touch against my own in a way that was instantly enslaving, and this was just his kiss. I didn't want him to stop. My hands eagerly clasped his jaw with a need to prolong our connection. The more we kissed, the more brazen I became. I moved my hands up to rake through the thick dark waves of his hair and pressed hard on his mouth, sucking his tongue and filling me with his taste of crush mints.

He groaned as he covered my hands and gently pulled them down before ending the kiss, and we both worked to catch our breath. I let out a shaky exhalation and lowered my eyelids. "I don't know what's come over me. I haven't had sex with anyone since my marriage ended. He had affairs."

I sucked in to steady my breathing. I cursed myself for bringing the past up, but I felt the need to explain my eagerness. It only made me more ashamed, and I lowered my head.

He cupped my chin and lifted my face up toward his. "He was a fool," he said with an edge to his tone that I appreciated.

I licked my lips. "A man with your experience.... I imagine—"

"Has no expectations of you, trust me on that," he said resolutely. "I want real, not a sexual resume."

That made me smile. "All right. I know I'm not supposed to be talking, sharing." I blinked up at him and worked to control my breath. "I'm just nervous."

"I understand, and I'll allow it. I know this isn't easy for you." Dane's eyes danced with amusement before he took my hands in his. "We start with you following. When you're in a bedroom with me, you'll need to ask permission."

My lips parted. "For what?"

"For everything," he said darkly. Dane's authoritative shift was heady. My inner muscles clenched and my clit pulsed in response. I was hot to experience his brand of domination, and he didn't hesitate to give it. "Stand between my legs."

I moved to my feet and positioned myself in the gap between his strong thighs and long legs.

"I've been thinking about you all day." He undid the tie on my wrap dress and spread it open. I shuddered as his hard gaze moved over the lace pushup bra and matching panties I had on underneath. "I imagined how hot your body would be." His fingers grazed over the tops of the clasps holding the garters of my silk stockings. "And how much I want you under my hand. You want that, Gia? Tell me."

My body flooded with heat as my pulse increased. "Yes...I do."

"Take off your bra," he commanded in a low tone. "I want to see how sexy you are."

My fingers trembled so much as I unclasped my bra. He unwrapped my dress and helped pull it down my arms and onto the carpet, my bra following next.

His eyes darkened as they stared lustfully at my nipples, which were hardening, already aching for his touch. "Your breasts are perfect," he groaned out, voicing his praise. "Cup them and offer them to me by leaning closer to my mouth so I can suck them."

I heated up at his words and did as he requested. When my breasts were within reach, he placed a kiss on each one then squeezed them in his hands, and I couldn't help but moan. Closing his mouth over my nipple, he licked over the tight point before sucking deeply, his teeth lightly biting down on one and then the other. The bite sent a jolt of pain and pleasure straight down to my throbbing clit and I let out a cry; it felt wonderful.

"You're so responsive to my touch." He blew puffs of air across the tips and I shivered, though heat waved between us.

His index finger trailed down my stomach to the top of the lace of my underwear.

"I was envious of Elliott, how Elliott teased me with the sound of how wet your pussy was," he said through gritted teeth. "How you asked for permission to get fucked by his hand and let me watch. Take your panties off...slowly."

I took in a ragged breath as I shimmied the lace and satin down my legs. I pulled them off and handed them to him.

"Fuck, you're stunning," he groaned.

I sucked in air as I stood there, exposed and trembling in front of him, my arousal slicking my thighs.

"All I could think about was feeling you come on my face...how good you'd taste. You made me crave you." His words had an edge, like he had reached the end of his patience. His hands slid over my buttocks to the tops of my thighs and he tugged them apart, making me widen my stance. "Beg me, Gia."

"Please, Dane," I pleaded without hesitation. I could feel my pulse pounding in my ears, and anticipation charged the air between us. I wasn't about to deny him. I was too far gone now.

He swiftly moved me onto the bed. "Spread your legs wide for me." I opened my legs some, but he spread them wider and then buried his face between them. His tongue was desperate and seeking as he licked through my slick folds with long wet strokes, pressing in against my swollen clit. The intensity of his need and desire was urgent and demanding. Loud, breathy moans from both of us filled the room.

My hands caressed the soft wavy hair on his head as he consumed me. Never had a man taken me like this. Never had I ever felt so desired.

I ground my hips into his mouth as I moved closer to my peak.

Dane pressed the flat of his tongue over my cleft and held it as I came, shaking. It was so fast and so pleasurable, I rejoiced and mourned that it was over, but then it wasn't. Dane came undone. He licked and sucked my pussy like he couldn't get enough, adding two of his fingers in, stroking inside of me, spreading out my climax, like continuous explosions of aftershocks. It was pure ecstasy. It made me too sensitive to the touch. "Dane...God...please."

He finally stopped and let me lie back on the bed. "I'm trying to go slow, but fuck—I can't, Gia."

I was dizzy, euphoric with the climax. "Then don't go slow. I'm sure I can handle whatever you want to do to me."

He averted his eyes and didn't answer. The moment stretched, and I didn't know what to make of it. Had I said something wrong?

Then he kissed me. His tongue tangled with mine, and I tasted myself. A passionate fluttering arose inside me at the feel of how good his tongue felt against my own, and even more so when he pleasured me. When we broke apart, his eyes held a weight that had my heart beating faster.

"What are you thinking about?" he asked.

"That felt amazing." My face went hot as I wiped at his chin. "Look what I did to you."

He let out a deep sexy laugh. "That's what I want, for you to be just as you are. I want you comfortable and sexually secure. I promise it only gets better if you're willing."

Our gazes fused in lust. In mine was my answer: *Absolutely yes.*

He kissed me deeply. My eyes dropped down to the unmistakable outline of his thick cock pressing against the front of his pants. He followed my gaze. "You want to touch me. I'll allow it."

I reached down between his legs and ran my hands over the length of him. He was hard as steel. He took in a sharp breath and removed my hands, but he didn't let them go.

"Before we go any further, I need to know how you feel about bondage."

"I've never tried it," I replied. "But I've been curious."

"I'd like to try with you tonight," he asked. "We can discuss how you feel about it."

I licked my lips. "The bindings can be removed if I ask?"

"Yes," he answered. "You'll give me a safe word and everything will stop."

My pulse picked up as his words worked through my mind. Safe word? I peered at him through my lashes and found his gaze fixed and heavy on me. "You think you might hurt me?"

His Adam's apple bobbed up and down. "No. I won't hurt you." His thumbs massaged the backs of my hands. "I want to tie you down to the bed, but I don't know your tolerance for being bound. It's a lot to ask since you're unfamiliar with bondage, and you don't belong to me." He lowered his head a touch. "The way I held you at the party, I sensed you would respond well to it. If you want to stop, we will. I just need your safe word."

There hadn't been anything he'd done that had given me reason to believe he would hurt me. He was careful and kind.

He waited for my consent, and I gave it to him. "Perfetto."

He grinned. His fingers slid between my thighs and stroked inside me. "You'll be thinking of me binding and fucking you every time you think of your company." My inner walls clenched around his fingers, sucking them deeper inside of me, and he groaned. "Like the thought of me binding you? Then I won't disappoint."

He moved across the bed and retrieved a box, and I could see it contained more objects than the four black leather, silk-lined cuffs he took out. He told me about clamps, floggers, paddles, and canes. It was a lot of information to take in, but I was curious, and I wanted Dane. I shifted my legs, and Dane's eyes followed.

"Never mind all those. I won't be using them tonight," he said softly before placing the lid back over them. "These"—he held out the cuffs—"I got before I came home, just for you. They shouldn't leave marks on your wrists." He fingered the metal rings on the outside. "These D rings, I'll hook up to the chains I have in the base of this bed."

"Just in case a guest wanted to try bondage," I mused, picking them up. They had more weight to them than I'd expected. "You got these for me? You knew I'd come back?"

He gave me a rueful smile. "You gave your control over to me naturally. I thought if you returned, I'd have you like I imagined I would when I first saw you."

"At that fundraiser?" I half-joked, but he only stared at me intently and waited for my answer. "Seriously, you want your first time with me bound?"

"The idea of you bound arouses me." There was that sadness appearing on his face again. Seeing it tightened my chest. I always hated to see anyone unhappy. Clearly something was bothering him. I wanted this to be a pleasurable experience for the both of us, so despite my nervousness, I moved to the middle of the bed in submission. My hands and feet extended toward the corners. My skin went hot. There was nothing hidden from his view. I closed my eyes.

"Look at me, Gia." I opened my eyes and saw Dane shudder, his face darkened with lust as he gazed over my body. "You have nothing to be nervous about. You're beautiful."

He lifted my arms above my head and locked my wrists together before pushing in a panel at the top of the frame where the chains he had told me about were hidden. He then secured me firmly to the posts of the bed. His hands massaged down my body to my feet where he cuffed and chained them widely apart.

I felt my body heat with nervousness, though desire was mixed in. Dane sat down and caressed my cheek. "I'm honored by your trust, and I won't fail it." He brought up a black eye mask. "This will free you more. I want you to think only of the pleasure."

"But I want to see your body," I whispered.

He immediately stood up and removed his clothing, revealing a masterpiece of carved, tanned muscle. I was transfixed. He had some hair near his navel, and lower. His engorged cock hung long and thick between his muscular thighs. He was perfect.

My fingers flexed, longing to touch him to make the moment more tangible, but the ties he bound me with held fast. I couldn't move beyond his will.

He then turned around; he had angel wing tattoos on each shoulder blade, but that wasn't the only thing there. He had several whip marks that scarred his skin. He moved to give me a closer look and I saw his back was puckered in places, like something had been pierced through the skin there.

I gasped inwardly. He must have endured a lot of pain to get those. It was jarring and at complete odds with the persona that had taken root in my mind. I didn't know what to make of it.

"What happened?" I whispered.

"At one time, I enjoyed suspension, being hung by hooks through my back," he explained. "I know the scars look frightening, but what happened was by my choice, a long time ago. They are part of me and my past."

He smiled but went quiet, and I didn't push him for more answers. While I didn't understand how he could get pleasure from the pain, I didn't have to. It was his choice, and he was healed. Therefore, I returned a smile that I hoped was equally as warm as his own.

He came over to my head and brushed his lips against mine. "Take a deep breath." His deep voice filled the room, and I immediately sprang into action to follow his command. I drew in and blew out as he secured the mask over my eyes, blocking my vision. Once it was in place, I couldn't see anything, and the reality of my state finally sank in. I was naked, bound, and completely at his mercy. I waited for the panic to set in, but instead I felt excitement.

I lay there, feeling his caresses as he moved his hands and lips over every inch of my body. The brush of his lips and hands down my arms...a tender twist of my nipples by his fingers followed by a soothing lave of his mouth...the sensual drag of his tongue down the surface of the skin on my thighs and legs. He touched until there wasn't a part left that didn't have his imprint. His focus was solely on me. He had placed me in the position to receive, to just enjoy myself, and surprisingly, I reveled in it.

I also became painfully aroused, yearning to come again. A brush of his tongue on my clit had me burning for more. I arched into his touch as much as my bindings would allow, hoping he'd linger, but his touches were light, less stimulating. I whimpered.

"You take what I want to give, Gia," he whispered in my ear. "You will come when I'm ready for you to do so."

Sweat broke out on my body as I tried to hold back from climaxing. The sensations were tormenting and amazing, and when he returned to the apex of my thighs, I panted hard. The light suck on my clit sent me to the breaking point. I moaned and shook in the restraints.

"Dane, I can't hold out anymore," I begged him.

"I'm going to fuck you now," he said, and my body clenched tight.

I then felt the slippery tip of his cock rub over my swollen clit. It had me moaning and arching once more, before his cock penetrated. He eased in farther, stretching my inner walls; Dane remained in control, not forcing it, moving his cock in and out of me like he had all the time in the world. His warm breath on my neck and the sound of his erotic moans made me wetter as I took more of him in.

He rested his weight above me and let his power of possession weigh on me. I didn't think I could become more turned on, but I did. He ground his cock deep into me, stroking right up against my G-spot. He had me so close; I felt my body tighten and I moaned loudly as my body begged to come. "Please, Dane."

"Don't come yet, Gia," he commanded. My body shook as I tried to meet his demand, but I was losing. He picked up the pace of his thrusts, rubbing sensually against my clit. I couldn't hold on any longer, and he must have felt it.

"Let go," Dane said, freeing me of his erotic hold. I called out his name as the orgasm crashed through me, my body gripping him fast as he pulsated deep, and his own release followed. It was thrilling.

I felt boneless in the bindings. I could only lie there as he removed the cuffs and the mask. He next massaged my wrists and ankles on the bed.

"I lost control," he muttered. "You make me lose myself."

I had lost myself too. I was giddy, joyous from the incredible orgasm. "Then lose yourself in me," I whispered. I was grinning in full exhilaration. Dane went quiet. Had my comment made him uncomfortable? I tried to put him at ease.

"I'm happy that we both enjoyed ourselves. I didn't mean any harm by what I said. Kiss me, please Dane."

His lips pressed against my own and then gently covered my mouth. It was so natural, the most incredible experience of my life, the way we connected. Whatever came next hung between us, and we both went quiet, my own thoughts wondering what to expect. I was certain I wanted to spend more time in his company, but would he want more time in mine?

"I know you didn't mean anything by telling me I could lose myself in you. I remember once or twice when someone said those words and meant it. It's always that way in the beginning." The somber expression on his face broke apart my euphoria. I reached up and touched his cheek to maintain the connection that had formed between us, but he moved away from my hand. "I'm sorry. I just need...to think." He ran his hands through his hair then stood.

My face jumped as I worked to suppress the hurt that came over me. I hadn't expected my touch would be rejected so soon after we had just shared something so intimate. Did he want to talk about what was upsetting him?

"Sometimes it's harder to let go and move on," I said quietly, my voice raspy. "There are times I think I stayed longer than I should have."

"Perhaps I have too," he replied. "You don't easily give up on those you love."

"Is that what has you upset now?" I asked gingerly, my voice just above a whisper. "Are you on a relationship break? Is she coming back?"

He didn't respond, so I glanced over and found a blank expression staring back at me.

I moved to sit up and pulled the sheets around my body, wanting more than anything not to be nude anymore. I reached down and found my bra.

He ran his hands through his hair, his eyes downcast. "You don't have to leave," he said, but his tone said otherwise. His shoulders and head dropped, and he turned away. Something about him was off, and it bothered me. I knew it wasn't exactly a rejection, but it was close enough that I collected my clothes and put them on.

"This wasn't how I wanted to end our evening," he said apologetically. "I'll drive you home. I'm sorry—"

"No," I interrupted him. "Please don't apologize. I had a good time—we had sex, and that was what you offered to me. I'll be fine." I didn't care how haphazard I might have appeared; I just wanted away from where I was no longer wanted. I quickly moved to the door.

"It's not like that," he said, putting on his boxers. "It just..."

I paused for him to elaborate, but he didn't.

I swallowed hard. "You don't need to see me out."

He touched my arm, and I hated how much my body warmed to his touch. "My behavior is abominable. I apologize. I'm not usually like this, but...being intimate with you surprised me. You were more than I deserved."

I cut my gaze at him. *It was you. He doesn't want you. No one wants you,* my negative inner self taunted "Yeah...well, I hope you work it out with your partner," I replied thickly.

"Gia, it's not..." Dane started then sighed heavily. "I wish things were different."

When he didn't say more, I gave him a curt nod and continued my exit.

Dane didn't speak again, but followed me to the front entrance. Honestly, I didn't need or want to hear his regret.

I had to give it to him: he had the charm. He was an amazing lover, but he was attached more than he let on. I was now sure I couldn't handle a one-night stand.

I left Dane's home once again, this time sure I would never get involved with him again.

CHAPTER EIGHT

Dane Westbrook: We need to talk and I need to see you again. Call me.

Another message from Dane. He had been sending me messages for several days, but I hadn't replied to any of them. It wasn't just his rejection and the blow to my self-esteem that came after having sex that led me to cutting contact with him; something dark lurked beneath his tailor-made appearance. There was something going on with him that he didn't want to share, but it had him shutting down after sex.

It all came after experiencing one of my deepest, most secret desires, and then I was cast aside for the woman who may or may not have been gone from his life. The only thing I could think to explain the way he shut down after we had sex was that he must still be in love with her. Why did he have sex with me? What I should have been asking myself was why I was so willing to give over complete trust and control to a man I had just met. While I had no intentions of ever seeing him again, I didn't understand Dane either. He'd gotten what he wanted, so why was he still calling?

Perfetto was what I needed and where I retreated. The building remained open over the holiday break, and I easily fell back into my work routine. Working had a way of lifting my spirits. Every task completed gave me a sense of accomplishment as well as a boost to my self-esteem.

By day two of my working vacation, I had charts, papers, and samples out on every surface of my desk and tables. I was so absorbed on day three that I didn't see the security guard standing at my door, or Dane.

I was caught off guard that he'd been let upstairs without my knowing, but then came a shiver and a leap of my pulse at his persistence in seeing me again. My eyes briefly lingered on him and I sighed. Tailored and polished from his black suit down to his shoes, he looked good. I thanked the guard and Dane walked farther into my office.

"There you are," he said as he lifted a bouquet of roses in his hand. His tone was soft, and just hearing it brought back the memory of our brief affair.

Me—naked, bound, and open.

Him—shut down.

I plastered on a smile and accepted his gift. "Thank you for the flowers, but they weren't necessary. I left you a message about the remodel—I won't be needing one. I've decided to go for a quick sale and move again. The house is more than I need right now." I cleared a corner of my desk to set the flowers down.

"I got your message, but I don't care about the remodel," he replied evenly. "That's not why I'm here—"

"It doesn't matter," I said quickly then gestured toward the piles of documents. "I'm right in the middle of a few projects right now. I didn't expect you to come here so, if you don't mind, I'd like to get back to it..."

"I mind very much," he replied, and that had me stopping what I was doing to look at him. Then I couldn't look away, and neither could he. The intense physical awareness we had for each other wouldn't allow it.

I flushed under the strength of his gaze as he studied me. He took a step forward and I took a deep, unsteady breath as I stepped back. "I don't want to do...whatever this is with you again."

"I want to. I'm not done with you," he said brazenly. "There are a lot of things going on, but what I have to say will take time. Can you come with me now?"

There was a gentle plea in his tone that softened me, making me want to acquiesce to him again. I couldn't allow it, at least not now while I was still feeling regret about how easily I'd given myself over to him and the way he had closed off from me.

I lifted my chin. "No. I don't have time right now." I went around my desk and brought up my calendar on the computer. "I have the second week of..."

He came around the desk and stood a breath away from me, but he didn't touch me. He didn't need to—he radiated a powerful force and heat that already had my body responding.

My pulse pounded hard and my breath remained uneven.

"Another day would be too long," Dane said deeply. "I can't stop thinking about you."

"You're hiding something," I said softly. "I just can't handle being with you, even sexually, if you can't open up to me." His flinch was miniscule, but evident. Before he responded, his phone buzzed.

"I must answer this," he said.

"Go on," I said, thankful for the reprieve and the chance to collect myself after his attraction had drawn me in and made me want to give myself over to him again. Still, I watched him walk over to the window. He had a slight crease to his brow as he listened. When his call ended, he turned to me and sighed heavily. "I have an emergency and must leave right now."

I nodded. "It's fine. Thanks for the flowers."

Dane came back around the desk. "We still have things to discuss. Please take my calls. I'll be in touch real soon." His fingers warmed my skin as he moved errant strands of hair that had fallen into my face. I had no words to give him.

He left as quickly as he came, and his presence left me useless to continue working, my mind too busy trying to think of a reason why I shouldn't give him a second chance.

After packing up, I made a quick stop for Thai takeout before journeying back to my home. I hadn't even gotten my coat off before my phone chimed with a text. Dane again? A flutter went through me. He was persistent. I took it out and deflated a little—the message was from Astrid. I groaned. Was she going to invite me over to help with more campaign stuff for her husband?

Astrid: We're back in town. Have you looked at the news? Dalton Pierce has been arrested.

DP Management was the management company we'd hired to handle Perfetto, named for its head, Dalton Pierce. My eyes went to the holiday basket he'd sent to me personally as a congratulatory gift for Perfetto's record success last quarter.

Suddenly I wished she had been headhunting me to assist with the campaign. This scenario was worse than anything I could have concocted in my head.

My stomach muscles twisted in knots as I rushed over to turn on the news. They were in the middle of a segment on New Year's resolutions, but the scrolling text at the bottom said Dalton Pierce had been charged with bank fraud, four counts of counterfeit securities, and five counts of money laundering. Panic erupted inside of me. Astrid was probably frantic as she waited for my response. I quickly replied.

Gia: I'll find out what happened. We don't have all the facts yet. I'll be working from here on out to fix it. Try to relax.

I'd told her what she wanted to hear, that there was an easy solution. I wanted to believe I still had my life savings and company and she still had her investments in Perfetto, wanted to believe Dalton hadn't mismanaged the company. Patrick and I had checked him out thoroughly, and he had an extensive, high-profile client list, including A-list celebrities. He also had a stellar reputation in the business. This had to be wrong...but then there he was in handcuffs, being put into the back of a police car. With all his wealth and connections, they would have to have something to get him in that car, and especially to do it on camera.

Bile rose in my throat and my body shook to its core as dread took hold of me, my mind already racing with thoughts on the implications of what this could mean for my company. My hands shook so hard I fumbled the phone, scrolling as fast as I could to call DP Management.

After a series of beeps, I heard an automated voice say, "Mailbox full. Ending call."

I went through the list I had—his partners, financial heads, even his secretary—before it dawned on me that it was New Year's Eve. No one would be there. The call waiting came up on my phone, and thankfully it was my attorney, Stuart Miller. I immediately answered.

"Gia, I'm in my car. Can I meet you over at your place?"

I swallowed against the brick that had lodged in my throat at the woeful tone of his voice. Whatever he had to share wasn't good news. I didn't think I could wait however long it would take for him to arrive. "Would you please pull over and just give it to me straight, and right now? I don't think my nerves can handle waiting."

He sighed heavily, and I paced as I waited for him to come back on line. "Bottom line, Dalton Pierce and his management company misappropriated funds from Perfetto. It will take some time to decipher the full extent as we wait for law enforcement's disclosure. I've stopped all the automated transactions that had been going through, and I will be filing a lawsuit to attempt to recover what we can."

"Will we have enough to pay our employees the next few months?" I asked, my voice cracking.

"Perhaps a few months, maybe five, but I can't promise you anything," he said then cursed.

Tears tunneled down my face and I took a deep breath in. "We have production costs, marketing for our new line..."

"The bank may be able to guarantee a loan," he said. "But, with the other ones you have, you'll be in a lot of debt...I will work on it as best I can."

I drew in a deep breath "Thank you."

"Now, there is something else that has come to light," he said cautiously. "The investigators on Dalton's fraud case will want to talk with you, and I'll be there with you. I've asked a criminal attorney to join us to cover any issues with the selling off of Perfetto shares so close to the announcement of his indictment. I will assure them you were unaware of the investigation into his business practices—"

Selling Perfetto shares?

I placed his call on speaker and frantically opened my laptop to check through the online holdings. My mouth dropped open. "What? I didn't sell anything. Obviously, I would have broken ties with him and removed everything he had control of if I'd known he was doing anything criminal. The only shares that could possibly go through without my personal authorization are the ones Patrick holds, but with our divorce agreement..." The screen in front of me showed shares had indeed been sold off. "Why wasn't I informed by the bank?" I carped to Stuart.

"He didn't sell large amounts right away, as you can see," Stuart said, and his voice melted into the background as I stared at the columns on the screen. While Patrick was holding out on our divorce, he was quietly selling off all his shares of Perfetto, bit by bit. I had underestimated his greed. He had put the stipulation in the divorce as a carrot that he would sell the shares back to me, but all this time, he'd been siphoning them off until the last transaction was completed on the day I had received the signed the divorce papers. I had been too giddy to check over to see if anything had changed. I had been too trusting. I was a fool.

Even so, what he did was so underhanded. I wanted to fall apart, but that wasn't going to help the hundred employees I had counting on me. "What can I do now?"

"I'm ten minutes away," he said. "We'll find a way to fix this." It was what I needed to hear to hold me together, but it couldn't erase the possibility that my company could now face bankruptcy.

While I waited for Stuart to arrive, I called Patrick. "You son of a bitch," I said the second he answered.

"Excuse me?" he said. "I'm in the middle of lunch. I don't have time—"

"We both know you have time for whatever you want to do," I said abruptly. "You went against the agreement in our divorce. You sold the shares of Perfetto that you promised to me."

"You mean my shares?" Patrick said, speaking over me. "I sold off my shares because my foundation needed the money to finance the election since you refused to help with the fundraising. You know how much money is needed for re-elections. I was within my rights to sell what I owned."

"You promised to sell them back to me," I hissed. "Are you aware that the police are investigating Dalton for fraud? You could get in a lot of trouble for this."

"My lawyer assured me that the transactions will weigh out legally in my favor," he said. The smugness in his tone was hard to miss. "We were divorcing. I no longer wanted to be involved with your company. The timing of the sales was purely coincidental. I wasn't aware of Dalton's transgressions—"

"Liar," I screamed. "Nothing goes on in Seattle that your slimy hand isn't all over."

"That's not true," he said with fake indignation. "You're bitter, and you mismanaged your company. That's on you. If I hadn't sold all my shares, that money would be tied up with the courts. It was a stroke of luck, that's all."

"The sales went through while we were still married," I pointed out. "You will have to give that money to me."

"You want money that is being investigated?" he argued. "It's already been spent toward the marketing for my reelection, something that wouldn't have cost as much if you had just made some calls. Now, I could help you stay afloat by speaking with your father's lawyers."

"You most certainly will not," I said. He would, without a doubt, try to find more money for himself. "You were the one who recommended Dalton in the first place..." I almost dropped the phone. The pieces were falling into place. Patrick had to have known. He'd fucked me over better than he had ever fucked me in our marriage.

"I didn't know about Dalton. I'm as upset as you are," he said nonchalantly. "I'd help you out if you'd help me. We can put this divorce behind us if you'll make some calls to get some of my previous donors to renew their annual donations. I'm sure I can recover some of your overhead, out of love and friendship—"

I hung up on him.

"Fuck!" My voice echoed off the walls of the practically empty room.

My phone rang again, and this time I didn't answer. I didn't have answers.

When the voicemail sounded, I checked to find that it was Dane again. I had too much on my plate to talk to him or think about getting together again right then. A moment later, I dialed my father's number before I lost my nerve. There was a sliver of hope that he might be able to help me.

"I'd like to speak to my father," I said to his private nurse when she answered. "How is he today?"

"He's quite alert today," she said in a cheery voice. "He'll be happy to hear from you. One moment."

My chest tightened as I waited for my father to come on the line. His memory had become fuzzy after the mild stroke he'd had a few months before. It had been unfortunate that we'd had an argument about finances before it happened. However, on his good days, he was still my favorite person in the world. That was how I greeted him, and he replied in kind.

"Missing my favorite daughter in the world," he said. Hearing the slight shake in his voice had the tears rising again.

I caught myself and tried to focus. "I had hoped you would be able to spend Christmas here this year. I sent the tickets, but your doctor advised against having you travel right now."

"You did? I didn't know, Gia," he said. "Did you tell me?" he asked in a cautious tone, and fear clutched my heart at the thought of him being taken away from me.

"No. It was going to be a surprise," I said, trying hard to seem upbeat.

"Oh good," he said. His sigh of relief was its own reward. "Now, you called about something else—I can hear it in your voice," he said. "You can tell me anything."

I swallowed, trying to work up the nerve to steer the conversation to the trust my grandma and grandpa had willed to me. I would only be accessing it eighteen months early. "Daddy, do you remember my company, Perfetto?"

"Oh, don't go into business," he replied. "It's a dangerous gamble. Most businesses fail in the first few years. I know you were upset at me when I asked Dad to keep me in charge of your money until you're thirty, but money is wasted on the young, and with the way Patrick goes through cash, you'd end up broke—or is that what has you sounding funny? Is Patrick in need of help again?"

"No." I cleared my throat. He didn't recall our divorce.

"Good, because he's not getting his hands on your trust, I made damn sure of that," he said then tutted disapprovingly.

I sighed heavily. There was no way I could ask him to help me now. My trust had been our last argument before his health failed.

As executor, he had convinced them to add in a stipulation to have it held until I turned thirty. He had been right about Patrick all along, though now with his memory mixing up, I couldn't tell him. There was no way he would pass a health evaluation to sign any release of money right now. I was on my own.

I wiped the tear that dropped on my shirt. "Did you like the Christmas present I sent?" I asked, changing the subject.

"You got me the…" He paused.

"The big band records," I finished for him.

"The music I love," he said. "Thank you."

"You're welcome, Dad," I said thickly. "I'll call you soon. I love you."

"I love you too, my sweet pea," he said, and we hung up.

A moment later, Stuart arrived in a Brooks Brothers suit, leather case in hand, to discuss what he knew so far. From his initial report, I learned my antiquated home and a few stocks were all I had left for the next twenty months. Even with the litigation, I wouldn't be able to recover the money needed to keep Perfetto running. There was no way my dad was of sound enough mind to sign the documents to help me, so I'd lose Perfetto. I dropped my head in my hands, despairing at my stupidity for agreeing to use Dalton's firm, though I wasn't completely to blame—Perfetto wasn't the only company DP Management had swindled. However, I prided myself on staying on top of the business. I didn't know what to tell Astrid and my employees. Would I need to ask Patrick if he could use whatever connections he had as governor to help me save it?

My stomach lurched at the thought. Then again, I knew what was behind his curtain—he had no clout. Still, shouldn't I try? I couldn't just let go of my company so easily.

"Perhaps the buyer would be willing to be a temporary partner until you receive your trust or secure another bank loan, though the market will make taking one a higher risk," Stuart said, breaking through my thoughts.

I tensed. "You're recommending I sell off more of my company?"

"Or you can cut your losses to avoid filing bankruptcy," he said bluntly. "Hear me out: we can make it part of the agreement that you remain the director."

"And Astrid," I added.

He nodded. "All right. Both of you stay on as employees with the option to re-buy in a couple of years. Perhaps the company that bought the shares Patrick sold off?" He brought out some papers from his briefcase. "The transactions regarding the private sale of your company are all with the same company...Incubus Nymph, Inc."

Why was that so familiar? I rubbed the space between my eyebrows and searched my memory, but the answer lay just out of reach.

"Do you have any more information?" I pressed Stuart.

"Only what's on this paper," he said, holding it out to me.

I saw the logo, and my blood ran cold as I recalled the first time I saw the image. The original sculpture at The Agency mixer...I had been speaking with Dane, and he told me the name...

It was Dane. He was involved in the sale of the shares of Perfetto, and according to the reports, the transactions went back months. He had known full well what my situation was before inviting me to his home...and into his bed. He was taking Perfetto, but why? I was going to find out and stop whatever sick, twisted game he had started, though I had no idea how.

"I know the owner," I told Stuart. "And I will be getting to the bottom of this myself."

I would stop the path of destruction I was on before it ruined me.

CHAPTER NINE

My fury and anguish combined with the glass of wine I had after Stuart left had me too frazzled to risk driving, so I sent for one of our pre-paid hired cars. The rain over the fresh snow made the journey slow. I was determined to go to Mercer Island and confront Dane, but my calls to his phone had gone straight to voicemail. What I had to say wasn't suited for a voicemail; I needed to see him face to face, to look in his eyes and find the cruelty I had missed. I needed to understand how I had been blindsided by his seduction, his command of my body, and how good it felt when he came deep inside of me. All that time he knew he was stripping away Perfetto. I had been a mere amusement for him and his friend to toy with. It wasn't enough to take my company; he had to fuck me too.

The bottom line mattered much more than people; that was what my father had said when I wanted to go into business. Dane was obviously no different, but he would find I wasn't going to make his takeover easy. I'd sacrificed everything for my company, and I damn well wasn't going to lose it without a fight.

My arrival at his gate turned out just as fruitless. It was locked, and his mansion was dark. He wasn't home. I deflated and opened my mouth to request that the driver take me home, but then I saw the path to the side of the gate was lit. When I lowered the window, there was a faint sound of music on the wind.

Another Agency mixer? My stomach muscles twisted at the thought of Dane celebrating in the middle of my ruin. Bringing flowers as if that would make up for taking over my company? No way I'd let that happen. My work and success were mine. I had sacrificed so much to build it. I didn't even know what or who I'd be without it now.

My jaw tensed. There was no way I was going to let him or anyone dance on my demise.

Ignoring the protests of the driver about leaving me on the side of the road, I exited the car and closed the top button on my pea coat then pulled my black hat down over my ears to deflect the below-freezing wind chill that blew down the path. Two small flights of stairs and I could see the wooden deck ahead. The boathouse was closed for the winter, but the party was in the tempered glass and stone pavilion near the shore. The music I could now make out was classical and grew louder with every step. When my boots hit the flagstone and sand bottom, I could see the entrance, and I hesitated. Anger and adrenaline were still propelling me to move forward, but my mind was now warning me that crashing the party would undoubtedly cause a scene. Then again, causing a scene didn't matter anymore. I'd lost, and now I was too far gone to leave.

Squaring my shoulders, I moved toward the open archway. What I hadn't heard were the footsteps behind me. Suddenly, a heavy hand gripped my shoulder, making me stumble backward. I pushed out to rebalance and turn. That was when I eyed the gun holstered on the belt of the bulky man standing over me. The thought crossed my mind as to why a matchmaking party would need armed security, but then his hand clutched my face and lifted it up high enough to pinch my neck. The jagged scar running from his temple to his chin was raised above his pocked skin. "What the fuck are you doing out here? Why aren't you with the other girls?"

I swallowed down the fear that rose in my throat and clawed at his fingers to twist my head out of his grasp. "Don't touch me. I don't know what you're talking about. I'm here to see Dane Westbrook."

He ignored my protests and reclaimed my arm. This time his grip was as tight as a vice, and his cracked lips quirked up on the side. "Let me set you straight, chickee," he said through gritted teeth. "None of the men here want you for anything more than sex. That's all you do with them and their friends."

I took a deep breath to fight back my anger. I didn't need his speech. I just wanted to go, but he wasn't letting me.

"Please listen," I said, trying to reason with him. "I'm not..." I sucked in air. *A prostitute, escort, or whatever.* "I'm a client of Dane's and came to speak with him about a business deal."

It was a lie, but right away I realized that wasn't my only problem. The coldness in his eyes silenced me, and the hair on the back of my neck rose. My answer was the wrong one. He wasn't going to let me go.

"How did you get back here?" He dragged me toward the pavilion and stopped at the entrance, pausing to press on his headset. "We've got a situation."

My heart hammered in my chest as the thought crossed my mind that he might harm me, or worse. I squirmed and kicked in his hold. All I could think was that whatever he was up to, it wouldn't be good for me to go away with him.

"Stop fighting," he hissed as he grabbed my neck.

"Take your hands off her." Dane's baritone voice cut through the night air. He had on a tuxedo and held a golden mask in his right hand.

The man reluctantly complied with his demand, though he stayed within reach so I would be easily accessible should he choose to take me again.

Dane tensed, clearly alarmed by his presence. He took my hand and moved me close to him. I went willingly, if only to be away from the guard.

I could not stop myself from being drawn to look at Dane, no matter how hard I tried. His face was chiseled stone, cut with rage. However, when our eyes met, there was a softness there that I knew was for me. I didn't know what to make of him or this situation. My mind flooded with disturbed thoughts and waves of apprehension swept through me. I began to shake.

"You must speak to me now," I stuttered to Dane.

Dane moved us away from the guard and wrapped me in his strong arms. A ripple of awareness danced across my skin at our exchange. There was a sensory retention that clung between us. Our intimate encounter had had an effect, and it wasn't easily erased. Even after all he'd done, I wanted his comfort right then, and I hated myself for it.

I stiffened, but he held fast to me. Leaning close to my ear, he whispered, "Don't respond to what I say to you. You can't leave. You must follow what I tell you to do if you want your company back."

"You bastard," I muttered, careful not to speak too loud, thinking there must be a reason he was speaking low enough that only I could hear.

"I am, but I'm also too close to what I'm after to risk losing it," he continued cryptically. "I'll do my best for you tonight, but if you don't follow everything I tell you to do, you will be hurt."

I trembled, and he hugged me closer. "I'm scared."

"I know, but I can't take you out now that they know you're here," he said. "This mixer's theme is pain or pleasure. You must be certain which one you are. I'm booked as pleasure."

"What do you mean? I'm not having sex with you again," I whispered harshly.

"You choose pain and you will get pain," he said. "And when I mean pain, I'm speaking of what you saw on my back." His words came out calm, but the memory of the brokenness had fear gripping my chest, taking away the anger I felt. The last thing I wanted was to be vulnerable in his arms again, but I didn't want to be hurt or maimed. I glanced back at the guard with the gun. It appeared I had no choice.

"I choose pleasure, but I'd rather not," I told him. "I will follow your lead as long as you promise to tell me everything."

His chest expanded against me. "Good." He nodded once then faced us toward the guard, who was eyeing us suspiciously. Dane clasped his hand at the back of my neck. "I ordered this one specially for me earlier. She was procured by Mr. Carmichael."

I blinked at him. Procured? Was Elliott some type of pimp? I wanted to get away, but a second armed guard joined us at the entrance. The first guard hadn't blinked when Dane said Elliott had procured me. Dane had a part of my company, and he had known me before I came to The Agency mixer. Had I been acquired? Had Liz? I had been a terrible friend, ignoring her warnings. At the time, I'd been too busy thinking about my own pleasure to stay away. Had she known this would happen? What was going on with her?

"But she said she wasn't here for the party. She said she was here for business," the first guard said.

They stared at me, and I could feel Dane's will compelling me to follow his lead. "I was told to ask to speak only to Dane Westbrook," I explained.

The guard dismissed me and talked directly to Dane. "That's not following the rules."

"The host gets to set the exceptions," Dane replied in a sharp tone. "She belongs to me."

I furrowed my brows. *I do?* I looked at Dane, but he stared straight ahead.

"Now, I've decided to send her to my house to await my return," Dane said before stepping toward the guard. "In the future, if someone asks for me, you get me. I don't care who you work for. This is still my place." The glimmer of hope that I could leave was quickly extinguished.

"When she is cleared by Mr. Santiago," the second guard said. "He's an Agency elite member, and I have my orders. I apologize for the disrespect that has been shown to your guest, but I will have to get his approval before she leaves."

"Of course you do," Dane intoned, but what that meant hadn't escaped my awareness. Dane had little power at his own house. There was someone else running the show.

My stomach pitched at the implication. If Dane had no control, would he be able to save me? Was there a way I could save myself?

My immense regret for showing up and disturbed thoughts filled the moments as the guard kept us standing there while he made calls. What I knew right away was that a negative mindset wasn't going to help me get through this. Dane wanted something, something he was willing to risk me to get. He promised me answers—*and pleasure.* I'd avoid any more intimacy with Dane as much as I could...*if I could leave.* The possibility was elusive.

An older man in a tuxedo approached us, and Dane quickly placed his mask over my face. "Hold it there."

"What is this I hear about you bringing along another woman to our special party?" His smile contrasted with his eyes, which were dark cavernous pits staring out of his mask. He studied me with an intensity that had me instantly folding into Dane, who placed his arm around my body.

"I was just about to send her home," Dane answered.

"Well I think you should bring her along," he said as he took my wrist, moving my coat aside. "She's doesn't have a tag, I see. I can take her off your hands right now—"

"I have her band with me," Dane replied, moving me closer to his body. "She's mine. I never said I didn't want her, I just wasn't sure about bringing her along."

The old man came closer to my masked face and his rough hand brushed against my chin. The breath he let out smelled of liquor. "Is she for your pleasure? If not, she can go with the group heading to Antigua."

"No," Dane answered. "She's pleasure."

"Then why not bring her? Or are you going to stay home too?" the old man said with a dry laugh. Dane stiffening next to me let me know he, like me, didn't find it funny.

"No," Dane said. He placed his hand on my shoulder. "I'm already set to go. I'll bring her along."

"If things don't work out, there is the trade show," the man replied. "Of course, there is a matter of price for bringing her in as a late entry."

My gaze shot to Dane, who went very still.

"I will pay whatever you request," he told him.

I scoffed. *He has to pay this creep because I showed up?*

"I don't like surprises, but I'm interested," the old man said. "She comes along." The guards flanked him, and he walked up a short path over to a few limousines that were idling nearby. "Let's talk, Dane."

Dane turned his head and spoke in a loud whisper. "Elliott, please get her out of here, now."

Discovering Elliott had appeared didn't put me at ease. "Quiet." He picked me up like I weighed nothing and put me over his shoulder. "Don't you say another fucking word, or you'll make the situation worse."

Once we were farther away from the group, I wiggled in his grasp. "What are you going to do with me? Just let me leave."

Elliott didn't respond, just kept carrying me up the path toward where more limousines were parked. When he placed me down, I noticed a few men and women filing out of the building. A driver came forward and opened one of the doors for us, and with guards all around, I had no choice but to get in with Elliott.

"Can you just get the driver to drop me somewhere?" I asked once the limo cleared the gate.

"You shouldn't have come, Gia," he said. "You're ruining everything."

CHAPTER TEN

When the car door closed, Elliott got the driver to pass him a mask. "You'll need to wear this. It's part of the festivities. The one Dane gave you was for the men."

"Where are we going?" I asked, not putting it on.

"To a party on a cruise, just outside San Francisco," he answered, motioning to the mask.

"I can't do that," I said. "Tell them to take me home."

"If you haven't noticed, there are people with guns," he said. "We don't show up, we're all in trouble."

My mouth dropped open. "But—"

"No more questions." He pointed to the window divider between us and the driver. "As soon as we can, you'll be on the first flight back home."

I followed Elliott's lead and stopped speaking. We arrived at an airfield and parked with the other limos then waited with a few men and women to board. They were dressed formally with Mardi Gras type masks. A few glances came our way with my informal attire and mask, but no one bothered us. They appeared joyous, a complete contrast to what I had encountered with the guards, though they were standing by.

I caught a glimpse of Dane boarding, but Elliott kept us at the back. The flight took off almost immediately despite the weather. During the flight, I declined any drinks offered. My eavesdropping on the conversations of the few men and women on board didn't set off any alarms. I didn't know what to make of any of it. Was it a masquerade party? I'd have thought it was if it hadn't been for more armed guards waiting by the limousines when we exited the private plane. The ride landed not far from one of the piers where we were all helped onto a private ship.

Once on board, we took an elevator a floor down, and it opened to a corridor of mahogany wood and Italian marble paneling. We stopped once we reached an ornate set of double doors at the opposite end. Elliott unlocked them and motioned for me to go inside, slamming the door behind us. Being alone with him didn't make me relax. Elliott, like Dane, was a part of something that included men with guns who forced me to go along. The only reason I could come up with was crime, and that meant being with Dane and Elliott was unsafe. Still, I turned to him for answers, opening my mouth to speak, but he held up his hand to stop me.

"Stay where you are and don't move," he instructed. "I'm checking the room."

My pulse quickened at yet another blow to my stability. I had taken his and Dane's word that he was an interior designer and Dane an architect. Now I could only stare, dumbfounded as he did a sweep of the spacious suite, checking the small lounge, the built-in dining area, the side lamps by the large custom bed, the bathroom, and the glass-enclosed balcony. When he was satisfied, he went over to a suitcase, took out what looked like a flashlight that glowed red, and set it against the wall. "I was told this will disrupt any video, but that's not one hundred percent. We are alone right now, so you can take off the mask."

I reluctantly untied the fabric holding the mask to my face and placed it down on a nearby table. "Will you tell me what's going on?"

"You'll have to trust me when I say it's better you don't know." He wiped his hand down his face. "The less you know, the easier it will be for you to go back to your life."

I didn't believe it could be so simple.

He sat down at the end of the bed, pulled off his bow tie, and rubbed his neck. "You may as well sit down." He patted the space next to him.

I tried to ignore the interest that arose within me at his beckoning. It could lull me into a false sense of calm when this situation was nothing short of frightening. I took steps back to lean against the door, keeping my distance to avoid falling under his or Dane's spell again. I also couldn't remain standing there, acting like I was a guest. "You can't expect me to just sit down and act like this is all normal. You and Dane are involved in something...illegal."

He gave me a hard look, his jaw clenched tight. "It's not what you think, but yes, there are things going on that make it so we can't let you go safely."

"Don't you think I deserve to know instead of being left in the dark? Tell me," I pleaded.

"You've gotten out of me more than you should have. Stop asking questions." His voice was strained, and I should have stopped questioning him, but I couldn't.

I walked over and sat down next to him. "You haven't said anything, and you know it. I need to know more. I want to know if anything you shared about yourself was real. No one was surprised when Dane mentioned you procured me. Is that your real job? Is this what you and Liz were arguing about at my house? You acted like you didn't know me when I came to the mixer—"

"At the orgy, I didn't know it was you," he interjected bluntly. "You weren't going to get involved with what's going on here, but then you showed up at Dane's house out of the blue." The derision in his voice intensified. "The Agency has zero tolerance for breaching security."

I snorted. "So this cruise is part of The Agency? I'm a new member, so you should be able to share what you know with me. Now, tell me why I can't leave."

Elliott sat there with his arms folded like I was inconveniencing him.

A wave of apprehension swept through me as I waited for him to say more. Seconds stretched into minutes, and each one that passed felt increasingly more unbearable. I'd had enough. "Fine. I'll come to the conclusions myself. Dane and you toyed with me, and the whole time you were scheming to take my company away from me. You forced me to come along in some sort of game you're playing to continue to ruin me."

"I don't care what you think about me," Elliott said before clearing his throat. "But leave Dane out of it. He's trying to help you right now. You made him vulnerable by making him stick his fucking neck out for you, and I can't even be in the meeting to help him." He cursed and wiped his hand down his face

The blood pounded in my temples. "I'm supposed to feel sorry for you and Dane when Dane's trying to take my business from me? I had no idea what was going on tonight. I still don't. I came to negotiate for my company—"

"With what?" he interrupted. "We already know you don't have the money." A chill hung on the edge of his words.

The hairs on the back of my neck rose. "How do you know that unless you've been investigating me? Is that how you procure—you look into my life for Dane?"

His nostrils flared. "I didn't procure you. I know it's hard to believe, but we've been trying to save your ass. Your name and company are all over social media for the Dalton financial disaster. You also listed your company ownership for the remodel. We could have easily found out about you."

"But that's not how you did. I don't believe you. Dane had my company before I even came to that mixer." I stood up and folded my arms. "Stop pretending to be a designer. Stop avoiding the truth, and stop holding me against my will. If your involvement is as innocent as you claim and you're really trying to 'save my ass', as you put it, then we can go explain everything to whoever is in charge and they can let me off this ship."

Panic rioted within me as my thoughts raced, analyzing my situation. I had gone willingly to this prison. Elliott was quick to take hold of me before I could reach the door, and I was no match for his strength. Tears threatened my eyes, but I held them in. Instead, I thrashed out with my arms and legs, making his hold on me tighten. "Let me go."

"Gia, calm down," Elliott said.

"You remain with me," Dane said as he entered the room, stopping only to lock the door behind him. He had the same solemn look he'd had after we had sex. "If we let you go, another man on board will take you because that's what a woman at this mixer is expected to do," he explained. "You'll also have to reveal who you are, and that'll be putting you out of the reach of my ability to help you."

I gaped at Dane and Elliott let me go.

My eyes darted around the spacious room. The Pacific Ocean was in front of us, and the door led to more guards. There was nowhere to go, no way to escape. There was the devil before me or the unknown. Still, I wasn't ready to give up.

I glowered at them. "You can't keep me. My friends, my company's lawyer will look for me. I am a public figure, a governor's wife. I'm active in the community. People will notice. You can't just keep me," I told them, but even I couldn't mask the uncertainty in my voice.

"Gia, listen to Dane. It's not safe right now." Elliott lightly gripped my shoulder. "Sit down and listen to us."

I jerked away. "No. I want to go home. If you keep me, I'll despise both of you."

"Hate me," Dane said before visibly swallowing. "Elliott is not the reason you're mixed up with all of this. He tried to save you."

I glowered at him. "What do you mean?"

"I will answer your questions," Dane said as he moved toward me, but I took a step back. "I'm not going to harm you. I need to know if the guard hurt you. I wasn't there when he first reached you."

His kindness threw me off and I answered without thinking about it. "I wasn't

hurt—except for when Elliott manhandled me."
I glanced over at Elliott ruefully.

Dane's gaze was unwavering, and if I
hadn't known better, I'd have thought he was
concerned about me.

"What happened to you?" I asked.

Dane's Adam's apple bobbed up and
down. "Are you worried about me?"

I avoided eye contact. "I'm not," I lied. I
cared. No matter what happened, I didn't want
me showing up to be the cause of trouble,
though what I really wanted was to go back
home. "I need to know what's going on here."

Dane sighed heavily and sat down on the
couch in the small living room area. "It's time
you know what I can share—"

"You can't," Elliott protested.

"I have no choice. The ship is casting off,
so she's a part of it now," Dane announced. A
tense silence filled the room.

It gave space for his words to sink in
further. Panic like I'd never known before
welled in my throat. I realized I'd been stupid to

think Dane and Elliott were the good guys and would let me go.

"We will talk things through, Gia," Dane said. "You will get back to your home, but you must first listen to me."

I sighed heavily. What other choice did I have now? I was there, and I wanted what he promised. "I'll hear you out."

"I'll go check on things," Elliott said, leaving us alone in the room.

I took off my coat and sat down on one of the built-in couches in the suite. Dane sat down and angled his body toward me. I had a déjà vu moment of the two of us on his couch at the mixer at his home, and just like it had then, his proximity affected me, making my pulse pump faster. That wasn't the only reason I was nervous. My gut said whatever Dane was keeping from me wasn't good.

Dane clasped his hands together. "As you know, your involvement isn't exactly coincidental," Dane said quietly. "Your involvement is partly my fault, but it doesn't start there. It starts with Angel." He paused, his breath seeping out slowly. "Angel—Angelica Browne—she...was mine. She is also the reason I'm here in Seattle instead of New York City. She's the reason I can't let you go now."

My gaze narrowed at him reaffirming his declaration of keeping me. "I don't understand. I don't have anything to do with your girlfriend or New York City. Is that where you're from? I've never heard of or met any other Westbrooks in Washington, and I've lived here most of my life, besides college at Stanford in California."

"I use my mother's maiden name, Westbrook," Dane explained. "I chose to do so after the scandal with my father, Walter Prescott."

I stiffened next to him. I had indeed heard of Walter Prescott. He had gotten into financial trouble with antitrust litigation years back by forcing his competition out of business. Public pressure had made his companies finance some of the midlevel businesses they had pushed to bankruptcy. "So, like father, like son, you decided to take my company?" I said with blatant antagonism.

"No. I'm nothing like my father." His jaw ticked. "We can talk about him later. That doesn't have anything to do with you."

I hunched my shoulders. He was right. I was getting off track. "Fine. I'll do better at listening. Please go on."

He gave a quick nod. "Angel came here to Seattle to visit a friend. Before she left, we had a fight. I wanted to move to a less open relationship. She didn't. She wanted to bring in a sadist dominant. We both enjoyed pain when we had sex, but her desires moved beyond my own. She wanted something more extreme."

"Did she hurt your back?" I couldn't stop the anger from my tone. No matter the situation, I didn't like to think of anyone in pain.

"She did, along with a few chosen friends, at my request, several years ago," he continued, his lips slightly curved upward. "I was experimenting at the time. Needles, whips, hooks—nothing was off limits. I wanted a bigger high. I wanted to up the stakes, but then I found my life was turning to chaos. I sought change. I met a Domme, a good friend, who helped me come back. I wanted the same for my Angel, but she wasn't willing. She came to Seattle on vacation and disappeared."

My mouth went dry. Sure, people disappeared every day, but with his wealth, surely he could've gotten some leads. "What did the police tell you? Did you hire private detectives? I'm sure you could've had the media at your disposal."

"That was what I thought." He bared his teeth. "However, her clothing design company was sold to a larger company for a fair amount. She had, on occasion, expressed the desire to do so, and no one around her suspected anything, but I did. The Angel I knew would have never sold it. She loved her company."

My mouth went dry. That was exactly how I felt about my company, and now mine was being financially mismanaged and bought out from under me.

"Her cards were still active and in use with no unusual purchases. The investigations concluded that she left." His voice broke.

I clasped his trembling hand. "But you didn't believe it."

Dane sucked in air. "No, I didn't," he said. "She wouldn't have left without speaking to me. Her friend gave me her belongings, but it took me a while before I went through them. What I found was an Agency card."

Stunned and sickened, I couldn't speak. I remained stoic as he continued to talk.

"You can call it an obsession or a need to know, but I couldn't give up on finding her. I expanded my company and opened an office in Seattle under my mother's maiden name. I made connections and became a member of The Agency. From what I've found the last two years, The Agency seemed to be more or less a matchmaking service. That was until your name came up."

My pulse jumped. "How?"

"It took about six months before I was invited to an exclusive Agency party for elite members," Dane said. "I quickly learned these men were the ones running everything. Your ex-husband had come for money. I'd say it was close to nine months ago. He offered favors, your company shares at wholesale, but that wasn't what caught the elite members' attention—it was seeing you in his profiles. Later that evening, I was asked to invite you to a party."

I swallowed hard. My hatred for Patrick had reached new levels and revenge took root in my soul, but there was more, and I didn't dare stop him.

His words came out fast. "I attended the fundraiser, the one I mentioned to you before. When the group asked me about giving you an invitation to join, I told them you refused, and that it would be better to leave you alone. Then a recent request came for you to join The Agency."

I blinked back tears. "Liz."

"Someone paid your fee before I could interfere," he said.

A shiver went down my spine. Someone—he didn't know who. "What did they pay, and did you have to pay for me tonight?"

"I did. The fees are one hundred thousand dollars," he answered.

My stomach muscles twisted. So that was why there wasn't a fee. Someone wanted me there. Besides Patrick, I didn't have enemies I knew of. "Do you know who?"

"I don't, but I won't lie, my interest wasn't innocent," he confessed. "I offered to host at my home in hopes of controlling what happened, but then you went to the room and you were everything I've missed these last couple of years. You were open, submissive, seductive, and beautiful. I couldn't resist you when you went into the green mixer. I made an offer separate from The Agency."

I lowered my head. "And I took you up on your offer for sex."

His face softened. "Because that was what we both wanted. I tried to pull away to protect you, but I couldn't stop thinking about you. I wanted to be with you again. I wanted to show you how good it can be when you let yourself go, but then I thought about Angel. I had shown her what freedom was, and I'd lost her. I wanted to warn you to stay away. I even called to set up a time to discuss the purchase of your company when I returned, but then you came tonight, right at the time I was finally invited to something more exclusive. I couldn't refuse once I'd joined, and if I even tried now, I'd lose my chance at finding out what happened to her."

I sank into myself under the weight of everything he'd shared with me. "I'm sorry for what happened to your Angel, but what does this have to do with me?"

"You came here, and they contacted the host," he said. "If you leave now, it'll be suspicious, and he may have you followed. I don't want you in danger. At least here with me, masked, we can keep you safe, and as soon as possible, we'll get you home."

It was a lot to process. I didn't want whoever was involved following me back, especially if Angel had disappeared, but I wasn't comfortable staying with Dane. "How can I trust you? You kept all this to yourself until I was forced to come here."

"I know," he answered. "I planned to and will give you back your shares. I'll pay off any legal fees you have or loans for your business, anything you need or want, but I need your help right now. I need you to go along with what is happening here."

My brows rose. "What do you mean?"

His expression turned blank. "This cruise is pleasure and pain. You shared your limit is pain."

I bristled immediately, catching on to his intention. He wanted to use me for sex. "You're offering the return of what's mine as long as I pretend to be your whore? I won't do it."

"And I won't be with you without your consent," he said with a sigh. "That leaves us with a problem. This pleasure cruise is where we test our new buys before what they are calling 'the trade show' mixer in San Francisco."

My lips parted. "Trade show?"

"I'm guessing it has to do with changing partners," Dane said. "Our host is keeping the details secret for now. As far as he knows, you are my chosen partner. They have all seen me with women and know how I am with them. Anything out of the ordinary will stand out and risk us all."

I covered my mouth with my hands. I didn't know what to do. I wasn't a child; I could handle going along with the game, and even sex if it meant I could walk away in the end. However, I didn't like how it debased me. I submitted to appease those on board in hopes of being let go.

He moved my hair off my shoulders, his hand lingering on my skin. The contact ignited an electrical charge between us. There was something there. It had felt real—until all this happened. He said the same. "We have been together, and when we were, it didn't feel like it was forced. It felt like a beginning."

I ran my hand over my arm. "It was a beginning. I wanted to explore and spend time with you, but not like this. How could I now, after you lied to me?"

"I didn't tell you about your company because I didn't want to risk them discovering the lengths I've been going to in order to try to protect you," he said. "Angel disappeared, and she was just as connected and successful as you. We aren't dealing with people who have no power. I will fight to keep you, but if you fight...you may be lost. I knew if I bought the shares of Perfetto, I'd return them to you. I'm now risking everything by telling you the truth."

My throat closed. "Why did you?" I whispered.

"I believe at first a part of me saw in you what I at one time saw in Angel," he said. "You both are strong, independent, and dedicated to your work. What I found on my own is that you have a willingness to take chances. When we had sex, I was drawn to your beauty and passion. We connected. I know you felt it too, and if I hadn't pushed you away that night..."

"Yes, I would have wanted to see you again," I admitted. He was right—I was genuinely captivated by him and had thought we'd spend more time together.

"I don't expect to keep you after what I've told you," he said. "But I needed you to understand what's going on and how we can survive this."

I flinched. Survive? This was dangerous. "For how long?"

"Five days, a week at the most," he answered.

My eyes widened. "I can't be gone that long. Astrid, my business partner, and Perfetto employees will be in distress after the Dalton announcement."

"There is a business center on board," he said. "We will work on a joint statement and I'll get it out to my lawyers to continue with business as usual while we work with the investigation." I went silent. Apparently, he had thought through this already, but it wasn't just work. I had my father. "My dad...is ill. I need to make sure he's okay. Astrid would need me to say something personal to her. She's our executive director."

"We aren't far from shore," Dane said. "You can text Astrid now."

I sighed, took out my phone, and found the battery was almost dead. "I need a charger." Although how many calls could I make away from land? I typed out a message to Astrid.

Gia: Hi Astrid. I'm checking on the situation with the company. I'll be going to my dad's for a few days. I'll have something emailed to you about what our plan is for now. Just go on as usual. Stuart said we will be fine to operate. Sorry I don't have the answers.

Astrid: It's understandable! That piece of shit Dalton tricked all of us. Do you think your dad can help? Just tell me if you need me to do something here. Take as long as you need. I'll keep you informed if anything goes on here.

He nodded. "I'll have Elliott check on your dad for you."

I frowned. I didn't want anyone but me looking after my father. I didn't trust Elliott. "How does Elliott play into this?"

His lips curved up. "He's a good friend. He will protect you, and that is why he will be here. It may be too late for me since I'm so involved with The Agency now. Once we port, he will get you out. I'll make sure he can help you and you have a way to reach my lawyer for your business."

"But it can't be too late for you, can it?" I stuttered. "What are you risking?"

He gazed at me deeply. "You still worry about me. It's touching, but you shouldn't.

What I ask of you is necessary until we can get you away safely once we port in San Francisco."

My jaw unhinged. I had completely forgotten San Francisco was where Liz had said she was going. "Is Liz here too?"

Dane rubbed the back of his neck. "Your friend made some poor choices, but I have been trying to keep track of her. I don't believe she is on the ship."

My stomach churned. "She's not in trouble...is she?"

His face went blank, his body still.

"Help her," I choked.

"I'm trying to help you, Gia," he said solemnly. "I've told you what's going on and now you will need to do what is expected of the men and women on board."

"And what would that be?" I asked, though I knew the answer.

"You will have to behave as my purchase," he said. He reached into his pocket and took out a black wristband with a lock on it. "You will have to be mine."

AMÉLIE S. DUNCAN

CHAPTER ELEVEN

I covered my hand with my mouth as recognition swept over me. It was the same as the band Liz had worn on her wrist when last I saw her, when she warned me to stay away from Dane, Elliott, and The Agency. Was she also given a proposition she couldn't refuse? "Why do I need to wear that?"

"The wristbands and locks are temporary," Dane said, displaying a small key in his palm. "It's engraved with my identification number and can only be unlocked by me. It informs any member that you can't be touched without my consent. It tells them that you belong to me."

My eyes flicked over to him. Something intense flared through his calm exterior and made a tingle flutter through my chest. The magnetic attraction I felt for this man hadn't diminished. Being his had stimulated more interest, and that would be my undoing if things continued to go wrong. I needed to collect my senses and approach this situation with some perspective. Therefore, I leaned back into the cushions and lifted my chin. "I understand the seriousness of the situation, but I'm not your property."

His nostrils flared. "To remain safe here, you will have to be. The men and women permitted on this cruise agreed to be kept by elite members of The Agency."

I grimaced. "Liz had one of these on, and I know she wasn't looking to be a 'kept' woman. She has her own business..." My voice trailed off. *Just like me.*

I got caught up in my thoughts and Dane waited. When I looked over at him again, his expression had turned thoughtful.

"Neither did Angel, for all I knew of her. I believe I'm getting close to answers. That means I need to follow their protocol and not do anything out of the ordinary. Until I can make you safe, you will need to be *permissive.*"

Permissive—the same word I had spoken to him what seemed ages ago. Too much had happened in such a short amount of time. Nonetheless, I knew I would submit to his proposed arrangement for nothing more than my own self-preservation. He was the devil I somewhat knew, and from all he claimed, he had been trying to help me. Besides, I wasn't a child. I could handle following his plan, even sex. Hopefully I could handle getting closer to him and keep my emotions intact—and my life. After all, this wasn't a game. Angel was gone and could be hurt or dead. I was going to do whatever it took to survive.

When he held out the band toward my wrist, I allowed him to lock it in place.

Dane exhaled deeply. A ghost of a smile appeared on his lips. "Would you forgive me if I told you it arouses me to own you?" He lifted my wrist, and I had no way to steady my pulse as he pressed his lips over the lock. I had no chance to hide from what he did next. His gaze swept over me from head to toe, noting the telltale signs of my body warming, anticipating his touch.

The shortness of my breath.

The swollen points of my nipples jutting out through the fabric of my shirt.

The shift of my legs to cover the inner clench of my sex, which already craved the thrust of his cock. Maybe it was the roller coaster of emotions that had swept through my life since he came into it—that, along with the memory of how good it had felt when we were together that first and only time. I couldn't let myself get caught up again. Though his plan would make it harder to keep my distance, I had to. From what Dane had said, he'd devoted years to finding his Angel. She was branded on the skin of his back; she was his love. I would pretend so he could keep his search for her on track, and then he would return Perfetto to me. We were each a means to the other's ends.

As casually as I could, I eased my hand back and stood up. "What now?"

He rose from his seat. "It's late and you should rest. I have to go out for a while. I'll have room service brought to you." He was at the door when I called back to him.

I licked my lips. "I don't know what I'm supposed to be resting up for."

"I need to make sure no one questions you being here," he answered. "You'll need to learn how the women invited here operate."

"And how do I need to act?" I asked.

"You'll just have to do whatever is asked of you," he said, a small smile on his lips. "Obey me in all things."

I rolled my eyes. *He thinks it's that simple.*

His lips twitched. "None of that or I'll spank you," he teased.

I rolled my eyes again and covered my grin with my hand. "Seriously, I'm not used to taking orders."

His face softened. "I understand. You're beautiful when you smile—I'll have to keep one on your face as much as I can."

He closed the door behind him and I sat there for a while, staring after him.

***

Neither Elliott nor Dane had come back, but I did find there were three bedrooms in the suite. I paced for a while, and the television had plenty of shows and movies. I tried to watch them, but I couldn't relax, so I decided to take a shower. When I returned to the bedroom, I found a face mask and a dark silk robe had been left for me to put on. My own clothing was removed, and a note was left that it had gone to housekeeping. My battery had died in my phone, but I wasn't getting any reception when I turned it on now anyway—more things to discuss with Dane when he returned. There came that flutter in my stomach at just the thought of being with him. I had to stop this insanity, stay focused on the way he'd hidden the fact that he was buying my company. He had chosen to let me think he was innocent so I would be open to his attention. Nevertheless, he promised to make it right. Still, what was going on and what was to come made me wary.

When I returned to the living room, I was still alone, but there was now an array of foods left in heated trays for me to eat. My stomach grumbled on cue. Though my nerves were still making me feel queasy, I forced myself to have some soup and a salad to keep up my strength. Afterward, I went into the bedroom and lay down. The ship was so large, I didn't feel anything but calmness on the water, and even with the turmoil going on inside me, I rested.

I was roused some time later by the bed dipping on the other side. I tried to remain still. *Dane.* Opening my eyes revealed his carved muscles in the soft recessed lights I hadn't turned off. He was naked and so close that I could smell the aroma of his body wash. My pulse jumped and pounded so hard I could feel it in my ears. I tried my best to remain calm and still.

My lips parted. "We're sleeping together?"

"Yes, we are," he replied evenly. "If we are to appear natural, you need to be comfortable with me. When and if we are in public, you need to be convincing to them that you are supposed to be there. You'll need to behave like you're not frightened and want my touch."

"But we already had sex," I said, though it felt good to have him next to me. "I even let you tie me up." The reminder and his closeness sent heat rolling though me. What tarnished the memory was how he'd reacted afterward.

"I know I upset you," he said on an exhale. "But for this to work, we need to start over."

What he said made sense, but was it all a pretense?

Dane's hand brushed down my arm. "I'd like to start over with you."

"How?" I whispered.

"We can begin by you taking off your robe and moving closer to me."

I eased my robe off under the covers, which he then drew back as he boldly stretched out on his side. Now that I was absent of covering, his gaze freely roamed over my nakedness, and mine gazed at him. He was glorious nude. My eyes dipped below his waist to his cock, which was semi-erect on his thigh, and I stared—too long. There was no way to hide his effect on me. The tight points of my nipples, the heave of my chest as I struggled to get my breath and pulse back to a normal rhythm. The slickness between my thighs and ache of my clit, which I desperately wanted to soothe. My mind was telling me I should protest, resist, fight, but deep down, that wasn't what I wanted to do. I wanted him to leave and stay. I wanted him. *Damn him.*

I curled on my side and scooted back a little.

Dane let out a low chuckle and tugged me until I was flush against the hard muscles of his solid frame. His closeness was like a drug, lulling me into euphoria. The brush of his lips on the back of my neck—so alluring. His thick cock pressed against my buttocks—too tempting.

I hated how easily I gave in to him and how much I enjoyed it, yet I didn't protest. I closed my eyes and took in a shaky breath.

"You like this as much as me," he murmured. "Let me see." His hand slid over my hip and between my legs, cupping my mound possessively. I shuddered as he stroked the wetness there.

"Dane, we shouldn't," I whispered, cursing myself for the huskiness of my tone.

"Shouldn't because you're upset again?" he said as he nuzzled his nose against my neck. "You're aroused like I knew you'd be. I understand and will do my best to make it right. I want you to submit, but when we have sex, I want you to come to me freely."

He removed his hand but stayed close at my back. An emptiness at the loss of his touch filled me. I groaned in confusion and frustration. What was going on with me? I didn't understand, but it had me tossing and turning. In the end, I would lose.

Dane would have me again.

CHAPTER TWELVE

"**D**o you realize it's noon?" Elliott said after shaking me awake the next day.

I tutted and pulled the covers up over my head. "Am I getting off the ship? If not, go away."

Elliott chuckled. "Ha. I pegged you for a morning person, but you're grumpy. Get up. I need to give you a quick lesson."

"What kind of lesson?" I grumbled.

I sat up and pulled the duvet under my arms to cover myself. His shirt was tight, showing every ripple of muscle in his broad chest and abs. His jeans fit just right—he was crazy hot.

He cleared his throat and my eyes shifted up to his handsome face, which was now sporting a smug grin. "You can stop undressing me with your eyes. If you want me naked, just beg."

I guffawed, but ended up laughing too.

"Good, you're getting past the hate," he said with a wink. "Seriously, Dane asked me to go over protocol for this type of party, but what I think you need first is self-defense training."

That woke me up. I was surprised by his offer, though the biggest obstacle could render my defense useless, which I was quick to point out. "I can't fight a gun."

"It's still possible to defend yourself, if you know what to do," Elliott insisted. "I'll go over some moves, but you will also have this." He dug into the pocket of his trousers, brought out a little metal square, and pressed the side, producing a pocketknife. "This weapon will be between you and me. Dane didn't want you to have it because he feared you'd end up hurt, but I think you'd rather fight than give up."

I dipped my head and smiled at the compliment, though I didn't feel strong at the moment. "Thank you, but do you think it will come to a fight?" My voice cracked.

He placed his arm loosely around my shoulder. "I don't think so. Neither one of us plan to let you out of our sight. We will hurt anyone who touches you. This defense stuff is me being overly cautious."

My chest warmed at his concern and when he leaned in to peck my lips, I didn't stop him. "I shouldn't let you kiss me," I said.

He cocked his head. "But you did anyway," he replied. "Don't beat yourself up about it. You want to kiss me, and I want to fuck you. There is nothing wrong with it."

I pushed back my hair. I didn't bother denying it, and his humor put me at ease, but I moved on. Slipping my hand out of the sheets, I grabbed my robe and put it on underneath the covers. Thankfully, Dane hadn't put it out of reach.

He handed me a tank and shorts to put on. "Such a shame to cover your sexy body."

My mouth dropped open. "I thought there was only a robe."

He laughed. "Good on Dane. There are a lot of things on this ship, including clothing stores."

"Then why don't I have clothes?" I asked.

He grinned. "Because we like you naked."

I tried to scowl, but ended up smiling. I quickly left for the bathroom to change. Both men were on my mind as I dressed and pulled my hair into a bun. They contrasted each other, but I found them both fascinating in their own way.

When I returned to the room, Elliott waved me over to a spot near the enclosed patio area that had an obstructed view out to the deck.

"This is how you hold the knife." He took my hand and showed me the way to grip the handle. "Quick bend to the knee to go lower. Jab. If you're close to his eyes or balls, go for it.

You don't fight fair." He twisted his body and lunged out with the small knife. "Now you."

Elliott was a good and patient teacher. He spent a good part of the day practicing defensive moves with me, both with and without the knife, until I was less shaky and more confident. It also made me more relaxed with him, so much so that it didn't bother me to return to the room in a robe when we separated to bathe and for Elliott to order brunch for us. I appreciated that it was one of those soft terrycloth robes even though its sleeves were a bit long and it hung just below my knees.

Placing my hair in a loose braid, I padded back into the main room to find Elliott standing by one of the windows, looking out at the ocean. The denim of his jeans was darker than the ones he'd had on earlier, and they looked even better. He turned his head my way, and I didn't look away fast enough. It was virtually impossible when he was in the room; he was just that appealing. "Nothing wrong with looking," he teased.

He would know—his gaze hadn't moved from me.

A bell chimed, giving me a needed break, though it didn't put me completely at ease. Someone was at the door. He gestured toward the bedroom. "Go put on your mask then come out and kneel with your head down and your palms on your knees." I quickly did as I was told. The only reference I had for the position was what I had seen in a movie, and I hoped it was good enough.

"That's sloppy," he teased, letting out a low chuckle in response to the curse I said back before opening the door.

"Elliott. This is the brunch you ordered," said a female voice in a tone that seemed a bit too familiar.

"Thanks. Set it up over there," he replied, his voice just as friendly. He was charming, but then again, I had met him at an orgy.

I waited until I heard the sound of the door closing before rising again.

The brunch was a spread of bagels, scones, eggs, steak, fruit, and yogurt.

I took the yogurt and bagel and was about to take off the mask, but Elliott shook his head when he sat down across from me.

"No, leave it on to get used to it," he said. "Outside this room you need to wear it and act as if it's natural. Dane and I have been trying to do the social stuff and leave you in here, but I doubt that will work for the whole week." I decided not to dwell on what was going on at the moment and instead changed the subject.

"Where did you learn those moves? Hardly something an interior designer would use," I said with sarcasm.

"Let's just say I didn't start out as gorgeous as I am now," he responded, buttering his toast. "I was a little guy in school. My parents got tired of me getting beat up, so they sent me to the gym to bulk up and hired a friend of theirs to teach me to kick ass."

I tried to hide a smile, imagining Elliott as a child. "Did you get your revenge?"

"Damn right I did," he said, and we laughed easily. "I kicked all their asses. I know that's not the right thing to do and people should do good, but fuck them. Once I fought back, they left me alone. So, you find yourself scared or backed into a corner, you survive. That's what I see in you, Gia. You came to Dane's with brass balls and didn't crumble to the ground when you had to come along. That's nerves of fucking steel. That's fucking hot."

My insides warmed at his praise. "You know, Elliott, if it wasn't for this situation, I might like you and Dane."

His smile wilted at the edges. "I hate that you're here. I had hoped the three of us would end up all having fun together."

I sighed. I had wanted that too. "Why do you even want to share me with Dane?"

"Less expectations that I'd be in an exclusive relationship," he replied simply. "I'm not the settling down type. Work keeps me busy and away from home. Most women want something steady. I also like variety in bed and want the same for whoever I'm with. Not many women can handle a man who likes to fuck other women, even if they get to fuck other men."

"Have you ever had a girlfriend or were you both sharing...Angel." I said her name in a hushed tone.

He hesitated before answering. "No. Angel wasn't my type, but Dane did share her with me a few times. I shared the woman I was dating at that time with him, too. What I mean by share is sex. We both enjoy watching sex and fucking. That's why going to something like an exclusive club was ideal. I can understand why Angel would try it. It seemed safer with all the privacy and medical tests."

"Do you think The Agency has Angel?" I asked in a hushed tone.

"I don't know." He furrowed his brows. "But Dane deserves to know. It's ruined him not knowing."

I agreed. Dane wasn't all bad, and neither was Elliott. "You're good friends?"

"Yeah," he said. "He's the best man I know. When I had an accident that ended my first career, he didn't think twice about helping me—he just did it. I'd do the same for him." He took my hand. "I know you're scared about everything that's going on around you, and I think you should take it seriously and keep that guard up, but Dane and I are not out to get you. We want to help you."

I bit my lip. I liked them both and wanted to believe them. I just was still unsure, but the defense lessons did make me feel a bit safer. "I'll think about it. Thank you for the lesson."

I stood up and was about to leave the table when Elliott pulled me onto his lap and captured my lips. His tongue slipped into my mouth, tasting mine. His kiss was sudden, and I was instantly swept in, kissing him back with my own eagerness and need.

He undid the sash of my robe then his hands grasped the back of my neck and waist as he pushed his muscular thigh between my legs.

I was caught up in the wildness of his dominant advance, and when he began moving, I was gone. He ground his thigh insistently into my crotch. The coarse material of his jeans against my skin worked as hot friction, setting off jolts of pleasure in my clit. I let out a moan and arched. My arms tightened around his neck, my hips grinding lustfully into his thigh, his mouth moving over my chest and breasts. *Yes.*

"Fuck, Gia," Elliott groaned as he pulled back, his chest heaving while he caught his breath. "We need to stop."

I climbed off his lap and cinched my robe back in place. My mind raced as I struggled to understand him, as well as myself. I was getting caught up again. This wasn't a game to me.

"Gia, don't be upset. I want you bad." He rubbed his jaw. "Dane and I are good with sharing you, and I'd rather we did it together. I don't want—"

"Me to have any expectations of more by being with you alone," I interjected hoarsely. "I get it. I shouldn't be doing anything anyway. This is an arrangement until we leave, that's all." I walked over to the couch and sat down, facing away from him.

"You don't believe that," he replied.

He was right; I didn't. There was a part of me that wanted to see them again.

The door opened and my pulse sped up. It was Dane looking impeccable in a dark pressed suit and gray shirt. His eyes shifted between us. "What's going on?"

"I wanted to wait for you before we fucked," Elliott answered. "Gia's upset about it."

My face burned. "I'm not upset," I said with annoyance. "It was a temporary lapse in judgment. I've come to my senses."

Dane and Elliott smiled at each other. Dane came over to sit by me and handed me a piece of paper from his pocket. "Here is the number for my personal lawyer. He has all the information I've agreed to concerning the return of your business."

I took the paper and studied it before putting it in the pocket of my robe. What he'd told him and the actual action plan wasn't there, but it did ease some of my tension. "Thank you."

He touched my hand, and our sensual connection flared. "You want to have sex with Elliott—"

"I don't," I stammered. "I'm just confused."

"Is it confusion or fear?" he asked. Slipping his hand around my robe, he grasped the lower part of my leg, making me shiver. Heat sparked in my core. "What we share right now is outside of what is happening around us. It's just you and me and Elliott enjoying each other. I want the truth. What do you really want?"

I shifted, and Dane's hand remained firm, possessive in his grip. My thoughts spun with how dangerous this was with the two men. It was tantalizing, rousing a desire I couldn't deny. "I want you both."

Dane didn't hesitate to act. He opened my robe and moved it back over my arms until I was naked then pulled me onto his lap, crushing his suit beneath me. He positioned my legs to the sides of his knees, exposing me to Elliott, who had come closer to the front of my body. His face darkened with desire.

Dane cupped between my thighs, his fingers sliding on the sides of my clit.

"I'm giving your pussy to Elliott." He stroked my already slick folds and spread me wider. "You want that, Gia."

I breathed hard between my parted lips in a low moan. "Yes, I do," I whispered.

Dane's command made me hotter. Our eyes staring down between my thighs at Dane as he teased my clit was going to make me combust.

Elliott dropped to his knees between our gapped thighs and devoured me. His tongue dragged up my slit and pushed inside me. He swirled his tongue and slipped in two fingers to stroke pleasure points. I was soaring.

My breath came out in pants. I writhed against his mouth. The ecstasy was astronomical.

I could feel Dane as hard as stone beneath me. He sucked on my neck, his hands kneading my breasts. "Don't come," he demanded in a deep tone. He couldn't be serious.

Elliott moaned into me. He licked and sucked on my clit while I writhed, my body tightening. The climax was inevitable and got closer with every skilled lash of his hot tongue. I quivered.

Elliott fucked me with his fingers, and in one quick motion, Dane slipped his finger down to my clit and pinched. The pain and pleasure hit me hard. I cried out as I came apart. My body shuddered as the sensual spasms tore through me. It was pure bliss. No guilt or shame came to mind. I went for what I wanted. It was sexually invigorating. I was ready for more.

"Mmmm that was sexy, but I told you not to come," Dane said in a low tone. "You came without permission."

"I couldn't help it," I replied as I panted.

Elliott removed his hand and stood. "I don't remember you giving Gia permission to speak."

Dane gathered my hair and pulled my head backward so I was forced to crane my neck to look up at him. "What kind of punishment do you think she deserves, Elliott?"

"I would say we should punish her mouth for speaking out of turn. As for coming without permission, I think she deserves a good spanking," Elliott answered. His pale blue eyes regarded me coolly while a hint of a smile touched his lips.

Dane knew I had limits and a safe word should things go too far. The very air between us was electrified and I was charged, so keen to go wherever the two men would lead me.

Dane groaned, placed an arm around me, and pressed the hardness of his erection into the crack of my buttocks. I moaned.

Elliott took off his jeans and threw them to the side. He was nude underneath, and my current position left me staring at his erect cock. He was glorious. He grabbed my head and pulled me closer then slid his shaft in slowly between my lips, gliding back and forth until he hit the back of my throat, with inches still outside my mouth. He stayed still, letting me adjust to his size. I inhaled through my nose and swallowed.

Elliott let out a groan. "Fuck, she's good. Go ahead, Dane."

Dane slapped my pussy with his palm and I detonated on contact. I whimpered, and my throat rippled against Elliott's cock, making him groan. He hit my pussy in the same spot again and I moaned, the vibrations from my throat making Elliott's dick pulse in my mouth.

"Breathe," Dane instructed.

Elliott eased his dick out and I sucked in air. Then, he slowly began thrusting in and out of my mouth.

Dane's palm came down again and heat lanced through me. His sensuous swats were making me unbelievably wet.

Elliott thrust in farther and farther, causing me to gag on his cock's large head. With every other thrust, Dane's palm hit my pussy, releasing pain and pleasure.

It surprised me how much I liked it and how the pressure was building once again. The men could sense it.

"Remember, you may not come without our permission," Dane warned me. "Especially when you're being punished."

I moaned around Elliott's cock. I was so wet I could feel it coming out of me.

Elliott thrust in again, making me gag, and Dane's palm came down hard on my pussy and clit. I cried out as another burst of pleasure exploded from the contact.

Elliott began thrusting in earnest, picking up speed. With every other thrust, Dane landed a blow, spreading the pleasure in my pussy. All the muscles in my body were clenched with anticipation, and there was unbearable heat in my crotch. Dane stroked my folds and moaned. "She's so wet. I want to suck her sweet pussy."

My inner muscles clenched, tightening with want. My clit was on fire from Dane's slaps. I was going to come.

Elliott kept feeding me his cock. I sucked hard on his thick shaft.

"That's right, suck me, Gia." He gripped my head, thrust his cock deep, and yelled out as he came down my throat.

I struggled to swallow as Dane spanked my pussy even harder.

"Come, now, Gia," Dane whispered in my ear as he strummed on my clit.

My body exploded. I came, convulsing, breathing hard, my chest heaving.

I was dazed when Dane moved me off his lap and onto the couch. He freed his cock from his pants and pressed the head against my entrance. My pussy was swollen from coming and even tighter than usual. I moaned at the pleasure and twinge of pain that came when he pushed slightly into me, stretching me unbearably. He pushed farther, stretching me wider, until he buried himself to the hilt inside me. Reaching down between us, he made a circle around my clit with one finger, teasing but not touching it directly.

It was maddening, intense, and I gave in to him as the pressure built once more.

Dane pulled out slowly, and my pussy tightened in his absence before he buried himself again in one fierce thrust that made me gasp. Then he began a steady rhythm with powerful thrusts that rocked me forward. He picked up his pace, stretching me and hitting a sweet spot deep inside me.

"Oh fuck, Gia." Dane thrust hard and fast, impaling me fully on his cock each time till he finally came, his hot seed erupting inside me.

He touched my clit, rubbing and squeezing until I orgasmed once again.

It was ecstasy, and I was spent.

Elliott pushed my damp hair back from my forehead. "We went easy on you today."

I was too tired to do anything but grin back. I was in bliss.

Dane chuckled then picked me up in his arms and carried me to the bedroom. After quickly removing the rest of his clothing, he moved me on my side and pressed kisses along my back then gathered me close in his arms. "How do you feel?"

I smiled. "I feel incredible, and a little tired."

He kissed my cheek. "I'd like nothing more than to hold you all night."

I looked around for Elliott. He hadn't come in to join us.

"Elliott is careful of attachments," Dane said quietly. "But I know he thoroughly enjoyed what we shared today."

I buried the seed of disappointment before it took root and snuggled back into Dane. "I enjoyed being with the two of you. That went better than I imagined it would."

"For me too," Dane said, and then he kissed me.

Things did get better, though we didn't have sex again over the next couple of days. The cruise functioned more like a vacation, at least in the suite. I was rarely left without Dane or Elliott with me. In the mornings, Elliot would give me some lessons and a lot of laughs. During the evenings, Dane would have dinner, watch a movie, or hold me silently as we stared out at the ocean. Both would leave to handle whatever was happening on the boat. So far, they hadn't returned with news on Angel. Dane didn't talk about her. Most of the time, he'd ask me about my life, thoughts, and dreams. One evening we were out on the covered deck, staring out at the calm black water after sunset. He had me pondering, of all things, what I'd done on my last break.

"Worked mostly," I admitted. "Running a business is full time, especially starting out."

"Yes, but it's useless if you don't take a break and rejuvenate."

"It's not always easy to take that time off," I said. "We have a pool to donate time to those that need it. I usually end up giving most of mine away."

"That's kind of you, but I don't agree with it," Dane said as he kissed my cheek. "Everyone needs a break. At my company, each person must use their holiday time. We've made it so that a part of our work incentives is to give away a dream vacation each quarter. People come back with a fresh set of ideas. It has been worth it. Imagine what you can gain from some time away, plus it gives your staff room to grow and learn to function more independently, before you burn out."

I sighed. "I hear what you're saying. It's more that I don't know what to do with myself...I haven't spent much time alone. I lived with my parents, roommates, and then Patrick. I guess I don't know what else to do other than work."

"That's understandable," he said. "I'm on the opposite end of that spectrum. I went to boarding school and I had my own place during college. I was always fine on my own, until I wasn't."

"Until Angel?" I asked softly.

"She was a part of it," he said. "I hadn't realized just how much she filled my life until she was gone. She always had something going on and was always pushing for me to get involved. She was always putting on a show. I tried to give her the space where she could be herself, or so she used to say."

"I'd have to agree, from the little time I've known you," I said. "You make everything seem easy. I guess that's why I'm not freaking out right now."

A knock sounded at the door, and Dane tensed behind me.

"Is something wrong?" I asked.

"No," he said, and we both heard Elliott answer. "If there's a problem, Elliott will come back and tell us."

A few minutes later, Elliott came out on the deck, holding up a card. "We've been summoned to tonight's festivities."

CHAPTER THIRTEEN

"**M**ust we go?" I murmured, but I knew the answer.

Dane caressed down my back and rested his hand above the curve at my bottom. "We do. It's part of being on this cruise. It's a chance to network, to show off the women and men they agreed to keep for whatever time needed. If they consider trading, it's a time to sample. All the members here agreed to it, or so I'm told, but...how do I put this?" He rubbed the space between his brows.

"It's also a chance for Dane to see if Angel is here," Elliott added quietly.

I swallowed and nodded, not trusting my voice to speak. I had forgotten his search for his partner. I also was having a hard time with the 'sample' part of the evening. "I don't want anyone else touching me."

"I know," Dane said softly. "And that will be my intention."

Intention—not a guarantee.

"Dane, you have to be real with her too," Elliott said, turning to me. "He can't stand out. Here you're a willing slave that will do anything that's asked of you without question, including letting another man see and touch you."

"With my consent—" Dane argued.

"And you'll stick out if you don't," Elliott cut him off. "You need to prepare yourself. If Angel is there, Dane will have to find a way to get her back."

I blinked. "Would that include bargaining me?" I tensed under his hand then rolled off the bed, moved over to the bathroom, and closed the door. I wanted to be alone. *Remember, you are alone,* my negative inner voice chimed in.

I didn't even get a minute of privacy. Dane opened the door and walked in, leaving it ajar. He came directly to me and stood close. His hands clasped the sides of my face, and I cast my gaze downward. "Gia, I don't know what to tell you."

"It's nothing," I said then cleared my throat. "We all had a great time."

"It felt like more than a good time." He turned on the water in the walk-in shower.

We went in and he picked up a sponge from one of the built-in shelves then took over bathing me. He was tender in his touch as he caressed each part of my body like it was a precious jewel. It was calming, but much too intimate. He could see his Angel tonight. He could be using me to get Angel back.

I stiffened. "You're preparing me to trade." I gave voice to my fear, but then didn't want to wait to hear whatever words he'd have to let me know how ridiculous I sounded. We weren't anything to each other. It was all sex. I went to leave the shower, but he took my hands and backed me against the tiled wall, trapping me. His hands quickly took my wrists and secured them in his grasp.

"You need to listen." His eyes seared as they met mine. The emotion and turmoil on his face was unconcealed, and his voice softened. "I will never trade you, even if Angel is in the room. Angel's been gone for almost three years. I want to help her, but not at the cost of you. Tell me what you're thinking."

A hot ache grew in my throat. "I'm scared."

I hated admitting my vulnerability, but there was something about the way he handled me that opened me up. There were moments when we were together that I believed we could have a beginning.

"I know you are, but you're going to have to trust us," he said. "Give me a chance to prove that I mean what I say to you." He pressed his body into mine. "Dammit. I came in here to talk, but I need to fuck you again."

I inhaled sharply at the contact. His closeness was so male, so bracing, and my flesh was still tender from Elliott sucking and Dane's hard thrusts, but I craved more. I needed our connection again. I prickled at his touch, already reawakened with need to feel him inside me again.

Dane let go of my wrists then took his cock in hand and rubbed it against my cleft.

"You need my cock inside you," Dane said in a low rumble.

I slid my hands into his thick hair and wrapped my legs around his waist. "Yes, please. Oh Dane."

Dane ground his cock in and pressed me into the wall. "Your pussy's gripping me so tight." He withdrew and then thrust back in. I panted as I struggled to take in air. He felt so good, and I never wanted it to end. "Come with me," he said firmly.

I let go as he moved inside me, hard and fast, crying out as I came. His breathing was ragged as he fucked me hard. He pulled out as he came, covering my mound with his cum.

When I came down, I went to rinse it off, but he stopped me.

"Leave it," he said. "I should rub it all over you to mark you as mine."

What he wanted to do was lewd and possessive, but if it made it clear that I was with him and he didn't want to share, I would leave it and let him do more to me.

Wow. What has gotten into me? It shocked me that I could find such pleasure in such uncertainty. My mind raced. Dane stayed at my side, touching and caressing me, and the more he did it, the less I reacted like it wasn't natural. I liked it. I liked him.

We finished up and returned to the bedroom. Dane retreated to the walk-in closet.

Elliott's eyes flicked over my body and his jaw tightened.

I lifted my chin. "What now?"

He motioned toward the bed. "All the members get specific clothes to put on, and Dane made an outfit selection for you while he was out. It came while you both were in the shower."

There was a black leather corset top with sheer bottoms and a thong with thigh-highs. Lying next to the outfit was a leather mask that appeared more severe than the other one. It had slits for the eyes, nose, and mouth. The back of it had a string to tie and a lock next to it.

My eyes widened. "I can't wear that mask."

"This mask covers your whole face and hides your identity," Elliott said roughly. "Some of the men are from Seattle. It's so you won't be recognized."

I scrunched up my face but started putting on the ensemble anyway. "How long do we have to stay?"

"I'm not sure," Elliott answered. "When we leave this room, you'll be expected to kneel next to Dane or sit down on his lap. You do not make eye contact or speak to anyone. I don't even want them to hear your voice. Whatever

Dane asks you to do, you do without hesitation, understood?"

I hunched my shoulders. I didn't want to, but I understood I had no choice. "Yes."

He bent down and helped me with the thigh-highs, smoothing his hand over my leg. "You need to stay calm. Whatever you see, don't react. Remember, we don't know everything going on yet. We believe everyone here wants to be."

"Don't worry about me. I'll be fine. I've got some moves," I joked, but my voice caught, betraying me.

"You do." He kissed my forehead. "You blew my mind."

My face warmed. "Stop teasing me. Seriously, I just need to know what is expected, and if all goes to hell, I'll kick ass."

Dane snorted, returning with a dark blue suit. "Elliott may have showed you how to fight, but I don't want you doing it. I don't want anything to happen to you," he said with a critical tone to his voice.

"And neither do I, to either one of you," Elliott retorted, his jaw clenched. Our eyes met; I didn't want to come between them, but I was with Elliott. While I didn't want to hurt anyone, the defense lessons made me feel safer. Dane didn't raise the issue again, so I continued getting changed. When I was dressed, I braided my hair tight to my scalp, and Dane helped lace the strings of the mask before locking it in place.

"Since Elliott didn't go over how you'd be expected to behave at this type of mixer," Dane started, "we'll need to discuss it now."

"You can't stand out or attract attention," Elliott instructed. "You'll have to kneel. You tried it earlier, but do it again for us."

I went down on my knees and placed my hands on my thighs, facing upward, my eyes focusing on the carpet.

"Hmmm," Dane said. "That's too provocative."

"Come on, Dane," Elliott said. "This is a show-off party and you know it. Spread your thighs wide enough that we can see your pussy."

"Argh," I groaned.

"You have on the mask," Elliott said. "No one but us will know."

My face burned. I told myself they had already seen me up close so I didn't need to be modest, but brazenly displaying myself before them was intimidating. The dark looks on both of their faces were enough to let me know I'd done it right.

"I'd say wider," Elliott teased.

"I'm not a pretzel," I shot back, and we laughed.

"Come on," Dane said, trying to suppress his grin. "We have to get the rest right. If you're on my lap, I'll open you up, but if you're on the floor, you lay back with your legs open."

My mouth dropped open.

"You open your mouth if you're kneeling between his legs," Elliott said. "Go on, Gia. Better here than doing it for the first time in there."

I grimaced but did as I was instructed, adding in an arch to my back with my arms up.

"Fuck. Don't improvise," Elliott said, reaching down and adjusting the front of his pants.

"Yes," Dane said. "And if I touch you, you don't have permission to come."

"Good thinking, Dane," Elliott said. "She's too tempting when she comes."

"Hello?" I said. "Talk to me, not about me. I don't think I can hold back if I'm touched intimately."

Dane helped me to stand up and kissed me. "I'll do my best to avoid it, but you have to try, or you'll be punished."

I grinned. I knew he was teasing, but I was game. So far, I'd enjoyed what he'd done when I didn't follow his orders.

"He won't punish you with something you'll like next time," Elliott said, bursting my fantasy. "Just try to follow our lead. You'll be fine."

The mask gave me limited vision, but I could breathe easily. He held me away from him, at arm's length. "You look exquisite, even in the mask. I know I'll have to follow the rules of the party by showing you off, but I don't want them to see you." He chewed on his bottom lip.

"I'm sure you've showed off plenty of women," I said in a light tone. "I thought that was part of your sharing."

"It is," he admitted. "But you make me selfish."

He looked mouthwatering in his suit. Elliott looked equally as striking in all black.

"Where are your masks tonight?" I said, my voice muffled as we headed out of the room.

"The men will be unmasked now," Elliott whispered. "Remember, anything out of the ordinary will attract attention."

We walked down a carpeted corridor to the elevator and took it one floor up. When we arrived, we were escorted by guards into a large hall. The room was not at all like I had expected. It was a ballroom decorated in a festive theme with strings of white lights, small evergreen trees, and floral arrangements placed throughout. There were men and women dressed in formalwear seated at linen-draped tables. Some were playing chess and cards while others chatted on lounge chairs and couches. It appeared no different than what I would have found at a party on any other occasion, though there was one prominent exception.

Some of the women with the bracelets were dressed while others were naked on cushions by the seats or being toyed with by the men. All were masked. Even with my limited view of the men as we moved past the tables, I understood Elliott's and Dane's precautions. There were several men I recognized in attendance, some among the upper echelons of Washington's elite. A few I knew had partners or were married and had children. If their secrets got out, it would shake our world. I was certain any of the men I saw there would harm me before leaving me with their secret. My presence there was dangerous.

I forced myself to stare at the heels on my feet. Dane and Elliott put their hands on my back and guided me forward. We moved slowly, giving Dane and Elliott a chance to search around for Angel, but then a gravelly voice beckoned us over. "Dane, Elliott, join us."

I recognized the old man's voice as the one I'd heard by the boathouse on Dane's property.

"We have our own table, Vincent," Dane said, his tone clipped.

"But we're happy to join you. Thanks for inviting us," Elliott added. I glimpsed him taking a seat on the other side of the half-moon shaped lounge.

Dane tapped my shoulder and I went down on the cushion at his feet, relieved to not be at eye level with the man, although I could feel his stare on me from across the table. The sound of loud slurps had me glimpsing over at Vincent. A naked woman was between his legs, sucking on his cock through his open trousers. A dry laugh erupted from him and I quickly lowered my head back down. I cringed inwardly. He'd already noticed me.

Dane petted my head, and I leaned in slightly to let him know I was okay.

"Get off," Vincent admonished coarsely.

The woman tumbled to the floor. His foot came down on her hand, but she didn't make a sound.

"She's well trained," I heard Elliott's voice say. "At least in keeping her mouth shut."

I glared at him behind my mask.

"She still uses her teeth," Vincent complained. "I'll have to remove them or pass her around to learn how to suck. You interested, Elliott?"

"I'll take her off your hands if you're already bored," Elliott joked back, and they laughed.

My stomach lurched. It was a good thing I had the mask to cover my face; there was no way I could hide my disgust otherwise. I hoped Elliott was joking.

"Dane, you're quiet over there," Vincent mused. "I see you brought your last-minute entry?" There was a slight edge to his tone.

"Yes, I did," Dane answered coolly.

"Drinks." A staff member came over, and the three men conversed about the holiday and business. After a while, my legs cramped from the kneeling. They were all absorbed in their conversation, like us two women weren't even there. So, I stretched. I quickly realized soothing my discomfort was an error when Vincent let out a derisive snort.

"Untrained I see," Vincent said. "What are you calling it?"

I seethed behind the mask at him calling me an *it*.

"No name yet." Elliott laughed. "We don't know if we're keeping her."

I tensed. Elliott seemed too at ease here. Was he really Dane's friend? Had I given in to an enemy or was he just playing the role expected of him? My mind raced, but then Dane spoke up.

"I call her mine." He put his hand on my neck. "That's all you need to know."

"She can't be just yours," Vincent replied, his voice flat. "She's here, and part of being here is negotiating. Now I'm curious as to what has you already owning her after a few days. Send her over to me."

"Why tempt you with what I'm not willing to share," Dane said in a curt tone.

"I bet you've been willing to give Elliott a taste," Vincent pouted.

"I had a taste," Elliott affirmed in a bored tone. "Why do you think I'm here now?" He chuckled, but Vincent didn't join him this time.

My shoulders slumped. He may have been playing along, but his words still stung.

"You come out and see all our secrets," Vincent grumbled. "But you want to keep your pet at the sampling party. Perhaps it would be better if you leave before the trade show."

"Now, Vincent," Elliott said. "There isn't a rule that says you have to share with everyone. Dane already shared her with me. He's keeping with protocol."

"Elliott's right," Dane said. "I only share with those of my choosing. I don't choose you."

Silence stretched between them.

"Perhaps it would be better to show her off," Elliott said, speaking up. "It's harmless."

Vincent coughed. "Thank you, Elliott. I was beginning to think Dane had lost himself. It was sure making me curious to see what was so special about her that has Dane so anxious."

"We can show you there is nothing to get upset about," Elliott said in a curt tone. It was an obvious warning to Dane.

I moved a little, trying to send my own signal to Dane that I'd do whatever he needed to keep the peace.

"Stand between my legs," Dane instructed.

I did as I was told and kept my head low as Dane undid my corset and worked my thong down to the floor, leaving my body on display for anyone looking in our direction.

"Hmmm, she's older, curvy." Vincent spoke like I wasn't there. "Is her pussy tight? Get her to bend over and let me feel it."

"You won't be finding out," Dane said resolutely. He reached between my legs and stroked the cum he had left there, and I quivered. "She only needs to please me."

My body trembled as I struggled to remain still and passive like the other women in the room. My only solace was that I was still masked.

"Look at the blush on her skin," Vincent replied, ignoring Dane. "Kind of a sexy innocence there. Let me see if I can get you to negotiate, Dane. I'll give you the building downtown, the contract with a redesign of my yachts, and a million if you give me the rest of the ride back to San Francisco with your plaything."

I tensed. There was no way I'd go willingly.

"A night maybe," Elliott said. "What do you think, Dane?"

"I'm not interested." Dane pressed his hand on my shoulder to instruct me to get back into position. I didn't hesitate to do so, though he left me nude. My mind was too preoccupied with the cavalier way in which Elliott was willing to use me.

"I don't know why you're being so insistent," Dane said. "There are plenty of women around here, or men if you want one. I've never shared with you before, and I don't want to do it now."

"And why not?" Vincent asked.

"Because you break your playthings," Dane said icily.

Elliott laughed. "Relax, Dane. Vincent's only *teasing* you."

Was he? I didn't believe it.

The music started and a stage was revealed. On it, a couple went on a St. Andrew's cross. The Dom teased the submissive with a vibrator. He then used clamps on her nipples and pussy, ending by whipping and fucking her. The sex scene had all the men playing with their partners, except at our table. Vincent, Dane, and Elliott stared at each other while the other woman and I remained on the floor. *So much for blending in.*

Finally, Dane rose and tapped my shoulder to rise with him. "I think I'd prefer to sit tonight out."

"Elliott, you'll stay and participate?" Vincent called to Elliott.

"Okay," Elliott said. "I'm game."

"I already asked Elliott to share with me tonight," Dane said. "Maybe you can invite him tomorrow."

We were about to move away from the table when Vincent called Dane back. "A million for the night, and you, pretty girl—I'll triple whatever he's offering you."

I tensed. There was nothing Vincent could ever offer to make me go with him willingly. "I already told you, she's not for trade," Dane said through gritted teeth.

"Everyone's for trade," Vincent said in an icy tone. "It just takes the right incentive. You're too blind to realize it, or maybe there is something about this woman that has you disrespecting me."

"You demand respect, but you insult me at every turn," Dane seethed. "You went against the rules. You can't make an offer to someone who's claimed. Now, I haven't decided what I wish to do, but it is my right to choose who to introduce, show, and trade. If you have someone else to present, let me know, but don't mistake my politeness for weakness. Don't try me again."

We didn't stay around for Vincent's reply. Elliott's curse as we breeched the door told me everything about Dane's exchange with Vincent. We were in trouble.

CHAPTER FOURTEEN

W hen we got back to the room, Elliott was quick to unleash his anger on Dane. "What are you doing?"

Dane unlocked my mask and I pulled it off. "I'm not kowtowing to Vincent," he grumbled.

"You do realize that you embarrassed him. He'll now make a sport of fucking you over just to save face—"

"And I was just supposed to hand her over for the night?" he mocked, his voice raised. "I don't give a fuck about Vincent. He may have been able to push the rules to get Gia on board, but I'll be damned if I'll give her to him."

I wiped my eyes and pulled the braid out of my hair. "I don't think he really wants me."

"He doesn't," Dane said before walking over to the refrigerator and pouring two glasses of water. He handed one to me, and I drank it down. "It's more to exert his power. I don't have to give in to him."

"What if he has Angel?" Elliott pointed out. "You got this far, you're not giving up now."

Dane drained his glass. "I'll have to find another way. I won't sacrifice Gia for Angel."

"Thank you, Dane," I said, glaring over at Elliott. "I don't know what you think you were doing by offering me to a man who breaks people. I mean, how could you?"

I hated the catch in my voice, but I stomped as much as I could on the way to the bedroom in my stocking feet. That was when I realized I was still naked. *What planet have I gone off to?*

I sighed heavily and went into the bathroom, this time locking the door and turning on the shower to hot.

"I wasn't going to let anything happen to you," Elliott yelled through the door.

"Just let him take me for the night," I yelled back. "Go away."

The door being knocked open had me incensed. What was it with these two men and showers? "Get out of here," I shouted.

I turned off the water, but not before Elliott came to stand inside, dampening his suit. He clasped my face, his eyes glimmering. "I would never have let it get far enough to leave you with him. I have a hunch we're close to the inner circle. Vincent might tell him about the trade show he organized, if Dane wouldn't throw it all away..."

For me. I turned to face away from him and ran my hands over my arms to stop the shaking. "If he took me, he'd find out who I was, and I'd disappear."

"Never," Dane said. He came in the shower and stood close to my side. "I'm not letting that happen. I'd leave The Agency first." Dane held my gaze as he stroked his hand up my arm. Brushing his fingertips through my hair, he pulled me to him until my nipples brushed against his shirt. He tilted my head back, leaning forward until our lips were only centimeters apart. I felt his hot breath against my cheek seconds before his lips took mine in a searing kiss. He kissed me with an underlying sweetness that made me ache deep within. I sank into it, giving over to the erotic pull of the sexual tension running between us.

Grabbing my hips, he pulled me against his erect cock, rubbing my mound against the hard ridge until all I wanted to do was climb onto him.

"You need to feel me again," Dane said, his voice hoarse. He removed his clothing and lifted me off my feet, aligning our mouths and bringing my clit in line with the tip of his cock. I wrapped my legs around his waist and lost myself in his kiss, tilting my hips until I got just the right friction on my clit. *I could get off just rubbing myself against him*, I thought just before another set of hands grabbed my hips. I tucked my head into Dane's neck.

"I want you, too," Elliott whispered. "I'd never let Vincent have you or let anything happen to you now. If you disappeared, I'd tear this fucking boat apart and everyone on it. I wouldn't stop until I found you."

"Oh, Elliott." I breathed heavily, the air hot in my throat, and I swallowed hard. I was lost in the sweet reassurance of his words.

When Dane let me down, my legs still felt weakened by the eroticism of the moment. "Go to him," he said with a firm voice.

In haste, I fell into Elliot's embrace, and he wrapped me in a tight hug. He planted his lips on mine and broke through my tired defenses. All my senses went ablaze as his tongue slid into my mouth, burrowing like a hunting serpent.

Elliot withdrew his sugary tongue and held my face to his. "Take a leap of faith with me, and I'll make sure you won't regret it," he promised.

Spellbound, I watched him peel his shirt off, exposing bronzed, muscled flesh. With easy grace, he drifted behind me, plastering his naked chest to my back. His warmth seeped into my soul, his arms snaked around my waist, and his tongue gently flicked my earlobes. "I want your pussy, Gia. Give it to me."

I turned to face Elliot, sinking into the brimming lust in the electric blue of his eyes. His deep voice stoked the heat of my flaming desire. Just the sound alone could bring me to climax.

"Not yet," Dane stated from behind me with a tone that wouldn't permit insolence. He ran his hand down my back, triggering shudders along my spine. "You know she has to beg."

I pursed my lips. I didn't want to beg, but before I could protest, Elliott slipped his hand between my legs, touching the insides of my thighs. As his fingers brushed against my cleft, I became a feverish wreck. I moaned and hung on to him as he began a wicked pattern, swirling his thumb around my little nub, working a finger into my pussy, going a little deeper each time.

Just a little more, I urged Elliott in my mind, trying to wriggle down more inches of his finger, but then Dane took hold of me in a firm grip. I couldn't move, too helpless and stiff.

The two men had me entirely at their mercy, and I was quick to realize Elliott had none to give.

He played me ruthlessly, his fingers teasing with feather-light exploits along my outer lips and light passes on my clit until I was right on the edge, aching to come. Then he pulled back with sudden cruelty, kneading my ass, leaving me high and dry, only to start all over again.

I groaned in frustration. "Elliot..." I hissed, ripples of unattained pleasure engulfing me. With knees buckling, I buried my head in my tormentor's shoulder. It was too much.

"Stop trying to control it," Dane said. "Give yourself over to us."

He fisted my hair and pulled my head back so Elliott could explore my mouth. As Elliott tangled his tongue around mine, Dane attacked my gooseflesh-riddled shoulders with hot kisses. My body, caught in the middle of two men, shook in a desperate plea for more.

Sensing my impending defeat, Elliot returned to cup my mound, working two fingers into my soaked pussy and circling my hard cleft with his thumb. His fingers intensified the depraved torment. The air became hot with perverseness, my body pushed further than it had ever been. I was slick with sweat and feverish with want. I cried for deliverance, begging for the two of them to calm this fiery storm. No more waiting. I wanted them both to take me.

"You're so beautiful," Dane praised, wrapping one arm around my waist, holding me against his sinewy chest. While his hardness rubbed against the small of my back, he tasted the sweat across my shoulders, taking my skin between his teeth to inflict small, sultry bites.

His hands reached around to grasp my breasts, pinching my nipples hard. I cried out, the pain he caused sparking more want than ache. I pressed into the hard muscles of his front and squeezed my thighs together. "I need to come," I whispered.

"When we are ready," Elliot told me, stepping back for Dane to take over. Dane knelt on the tile before me and parted my thighs. His hot breath touched my wet pussy, and I squirmed on my feet. A low, decadent moan breezed from his lips. My breathing became ragged after he licked along my slick flesh, my clit stiff against the edge of his tongue.

"Don't come yet," he purred. He'd lost his mind.

I tried to move back, but Elliott had a hold of me. Dane pushed my thighs wider and probed his tongue deeper. I moaned, my fingers digging into Elliott's arms as Dane licked the wetness between my legs. In torturous strokes, he lapped and sucked my essence until it trickled down his extended tongue and down his chin. I bit my lip hard trying to hold back my climax, but I could feel myself breaking. Dane must have felt it too. He moved to stand.

"No," I cried out. I couldn't take any more. My vision blurred with unshed tears until I heard Dane's soothing voice. "You did great, Gia. Touch me." The smile on his lips looked wicked as he guided his engorged cock closer to where we stood.

I reached for him eagerly, wrapping one hand around his throbbing shaft and squeezing. With my other hand, I cupped his balls, rolling them in my hand. I stroked as I watched, wanting him to feel just as turned on as I was by touching him. With every glide of my hand, his handsome face tightened into sharp angles, his pupils dilating with lust.

"Yes, just...fuck, just like that," he groaned. He tilted his hand and I worked him harder, caressing and stroking him until let go, and with a loud groan, he exploded, his come projecting over me. Without any self-consciousness, I licked his seed off my fingers.

He kissed my lips then nodded toward Elliott, who was sitting at the bottom. A silent, almost telepathic understanding passed between them.

As my body shivered with suspense, Elliott went to one of the built-in cabinets in the room and returned with a small bottle. "This should make it go easier for you." He kissed my cheek. They were ready for me. Dane swung me into his arms and carried me to the bed.

Elliott settled on the duvet, and Dane transferred me to him. I thought that was my signal to take over and took advantage, straddling Elliot after arousing him to complete fullness again. So greedy with need, I mounted his awakened cock. When his veiny member nudged through the swollen lips of my sex, my opening closed on his throbbing length and I moaned loudly. The sensation was exquisite, but Elliott wasn't having it. He held my hips in place. "Stop, Gia," Elliot warned. "If you begin now, you won't get the pleasure of both our cocks inside you."

I whimpered.

"Soon, Gia," Dane said to me. "Suck my cock and make me hard again."

I turned my head, finding him stroking his shaft beside me. I leaned slightly forward, taking his length in my mouth. Dane moaned and held my head, his cock growing with every slow glide across my tongue. Elliott was still inside me, and he let out a grunt as my inner walls contracted around his shaft. "You feel so fucking good Gia."

I gagged as Dane thickened in my mouth. He pushed for me to take more, his shaft tunneling to the back of my throat. I struggled, inhaling through my nostrils, his sexy scent making me wetter. He pulled out and rubbed his cock against my lips. My tongue ran over the spongy tip, tasting the sweet saltiness of him.

Longing for that much-needed friction deep in my sex, I tried to move my hips on Elliot's cock, but he denied my relief by holding me still with gentle force.

Losing the fight below, I took out my frustration on Dane's manhood, sucking harder as my cheeks hollowed. Then his hand seized my head. I thought he'd exert pressure to control the pace of my frantic bobbing, but he only let his hand rest there. Now I allowed my teeth to scrape the sensitive skin, my hand to tighten on his balls.

"Fuck," Dane grunted, removing his cock from my mouth. He took the bottle and moved behind me then pressed himself against my back. "Do it now."

"Kiss me, Gia." Elliott's arms brought me down and molded his lips to mine, his cock still buried deep.

My heart pounded hard against my rib cage. The anticipation was too much.

From the bottle in Dane's hands, a cool fluid dripped between my ass cheeks. Back and forth his finger glided, drawing little circles around the rim of my opening. Without warning, he pushed in.

I tensed, bracing myself for pain, but it didn't come as much as I'd expected it to. Now it was more like a fantasy. I was sensuously trapped between these magnificent men.

"Try to relax," Dane instructed.

When he disengaged his fingers, I felt a sensitive void immediately. Dane then slathered a generous coating of that cold fluid then pressed against my tiny opening again, this time with his cock. I struggled then surrendered to the fullness, giving in to the new erotic sensations flowing from the slow thrust of his cock as he fucked me.

"You like it," Dane teased as he moved inside my back entrance.

I moaned for him. They had broken apart my natural barriers. Between them I felt vulnerable, but surprisingly content. As I relaxed, my arousal increased. I moaned loudly as my inner walls clenched.

"Fuck her now, Elliott," Dane commanded.

I gripped the duvet tight. The feeling was so intense; I wasn't sure I could take it. I began to pant as they alternated their strokes, slowly impaling me with precision. I wanted to move, but they had me wedged so tightly between them. The leisurely, synchronized rhythm of their movements reached my sensual limits. I couldn't take any more. I writhed between them.

"You stay right where you are, Gia," Elliott said in a low tone, groaning in ethereal bliss.

"Please, I need you deeper," I begged.

"Oh, we will, but first we want to savor your heat and tightness," explained Dane.

I obeyed with pitiful sullenness as they drew out terribly slow thrusts and withdrawals until I floated in a state of heightened arousal. I tried to concentrate, tried to feel each distinct cock inside me, but I couldn't. They worked together expertly. My nerve endings snapped with sensation while my abdomen tightened with expectation.

I gripped Elliott's shoulder with one hand while my other reached behind for Dane's hip. Grabbing him, I dug my nails into his skin; I was rewarded with a hard thrust forward.

Dane's hand slid from my back to fist my damp hair and pulled to assert dominance. Painlessly, he got his point across: I was under their command.

As if realizing the depth of my need, they began to move faster, sweat forming and coating us all. They began to move with wicked coordination, astounding me. Elliot's pupils dilated as he eased full tilt into the sweet warmth of my tight channel. My wetness encased him in a vice-like entrapment. Then came the jolting vibrations from Dane in my buttocks. I quivered and moaned loudly. It was ecstasy.

With accelerating breaths, the sex became a fierce affair of desperate thrusts. I lapped at Elliott's shoulder; the taste of him was intoxicating. His chin lifted, and I knew he needed my mouth there. Licking the hollow of his throat, I sank my teeth into his flesh.

"Oh, fuck yes," Elliott cried out. He moaned as I squeezed around his shaft.

Behind me, Dane went full blast with his thrusts. His cock throbbed in my tight passage then his wicked invasion became a slow but melodious gyration. Separated and stretched, I gave in to the mixture of pain and pleasure that erupted at each hard thrust.

Together, they moved inside of me, building a tidal wave I couldn't hold back any longer. I came apart as it enveloped me. I cried out, over and over again, unable to handle the intense pleasure that engulfed me body and soul.

They didn't stop. My heated pussy rippled around Elliot's cock, and my ass contained Dane's devastating girth. I took them both, wanting every inch they had to offer. I shut my eyelids to savor the electrifying sweetness that came with my surrender to being a vessel for their satisfaction.

Dane drove himself all the way in, his cock finally meeting that yearning inside me. A primordial scream came from my lips. I wiggled against his hard cock, letting out a sharp cry. I was surprised to find I was close to orgasm again.

"Let go, Gia," Elliot ordered. A sinister light danced in his pale blue eyes as he took my nipples between his teeth.

Writhing and shrieking between their relentless thrusts, I felt that painful heat settling into my lower stomach. I lost control of my body, convulsing and giving in to an intense orgasm. All I could do was gasp for breath as waves of release washed over my whole body. I shook with the force of my release, jerking and gasping.

Elliot yelled out his release soon after. Letting out a harsh groan, his hot seed burned within me. His body shook beneath me as he continued to pump into me.

"Gia," Dane called out as he lunged forward one final time, burying his cock deep into my ass. The force of his release and Elliott's thrust triggered a continuous flow to my orgasm, making my whole body shake. The pleasure was endless. I was left spent between their bodies. I fell into sleep almost immediately.

When I awoke, it was Dane's face that filled my vision. "You're back," he said. "How do you feel?"

I smiled. "I feel...amazing...exhausted. I enjoyed it so much."

"I'm glad," he said. "There is so much more I'd love to show you." What he didn't say was *if only things were different*, but I read his thoughts like he had read my lust. *If he wasn't searching for Angel and I hadn't come to The Agency...* Still, a little hope rooted in me as I snuggled between the men. The sex had been incredible, but it wasn't just the unusual lovemaking that really shook me to my core. Being with both of them hadn't been awkward. They both made me feel comfortable, attractive, desired; it was so heartening. Moreover, in the lusty depths of our minds, there was no saying where I could go from there.

Elliott left for his room to shower, and Dane and I bathed in the bathroom together. I didn't know what to make of it, but Dane wouldn't let me worry. He ordered me the most ridiculous sundae that had me euphoric at the end of my bowl.

I moaned. "That was delicious." I looked up and found Dane staring at me with the strangest expression on his face. "Are you all right?"

He tilted his head and sighed. "I'm confused. I've never lost control like that. I've been to a number of parties over the years, in different circles of The Agency, but I've never had a problem with participating or sampling. I've swapped with a few men there, but tonight I lost control of myself and became possessive. That was new for me."

I shivered. "I didn't want them to either. Vincent's creepy. I also recognized at least five of the men there from campaigning, outreach, and business initiatives. If you had given me over, I don't think they would have called my ex to exchange me for a political favor. He'd be looking for more help for himself. I now understand how much you risked helping me."

"You're still here." He ran his hand through his hair. "That's what worries me. I need to get you off this ship as soon as possible. There may be a chance very soon. Elliott and I will discuss it. I'd never forgive myself if you ended up hurt.

I touched his hand. "Can you leave too? I mean, you didn't see Angel tonight."

The corners of his mouth turned down. "No. I had hoped I would, but she wasn't here. I still have another chance at the mixer in San Francisco. If I don't find her there, I should probably let her go."

I bit the inside of my cheek. It was clear he still wasn't ready to do so. "I hope you find her."

He smiled. "Let's not talk about that. I've been meaning to tell you I started a sculpture of you."

My lips parted. "You did? I'd love to see it."

His smile was innocent. "Yes. You inspired me. I started it after our first time together. I couldn't stop thinking of you. Maybe...maybe I can get you to sit for me one day, once things are settled with your company."

"I'd like that," I said, and I meant it. "I can honestly say I'm looking forward to getting back to work, if thinks work out."

"They will," Dane assured me.

I sighed heavily. "Good, because I can't lose Perfetto."

"This is all for your company?" he asked, moving me into his lap.

"Dane," I whined, but I relaxed against him, and he laughed.

"I forget I should ask to touch you, but I just get a feeling and go for it." A small smile formed on his lips. "Now tell me more about why you'd risk everything for your company."

"Honestly, I hadn't thought I'd ever need to," I replied. "But I wouldn't just give it up without doing everything I could to save it. It

326

was always my dream to own my own company. I studied business in college and was at the top of my class. Even with all that, I started small. I worked every position. I wanted to know what it felt like. I sat in on every hire. I wanted to build a community in my team, and that's what it is. The investment each employee puts into Perfetto warms my heart. It's more than a company—they are my family."

He cocked a brow. "You're passionate, and an idealist."

"I am," I agreed unapologetically. "That was the thing that saved me in politics, before Patrick went wishy-washy with his policies. He wanted to change the world for the better. He wanted to make the state of Washington the model for the country of what could go right if we all worked together."

"I suppose a lot of people start with dreams and find themselves compromised," he said softly. "I've been fortunate in that my family has wealth and good stable investments, but I hate what my father did to get that wealth, and I try to do things differently. I try to support startups and help small businesses."

I chewed on my lip. "Do you think Vincent will leave me alone?"

"He won't have a choice," Dane assured me. "When we port, Elliott will take you off the ship. My lawyer will handle the rest. It will all work out."

I nodded and yawned.

"You're tired," he said, scooping me up. "Let's go to sleep." He laid me on the bed and sat down on the edge.

I gently touched the broken skin on his back. "Was it painful?"

"It was, but there was pleasure too," Dane replied softly.

"Will you be okay?" I whispered when he placed me on top of his warm body.

"Don't worry about me," he said kindly. "You leave, and if I disappear, it means it's even more dangerous for you. Don't look for me."

A pang went through my chest. That wouldn't sit right with me.

Right then I knew I wouldn't just walk away. I'd try to take Dane with us when it came time to go.

***

The pounding on the door pulled me out of sleep. The night seeped through the blinds, prompting me to turn on the lamp to see. I was alone in bed, and from a brush of my hand over the cold sheets next to me and the silence and lights out in the suite, I knew Dane and Elliott had left and may have been gone for a while. Where they'd gone, I didn't know. I expected they'd gone to smooth things over with Vincent after the confrontation the previous night.

The whole night hadn't been lost though. I touched my face and smiled. Me, Gia Ruiz, having sex with two men—and not just any two men, Dane and Elliott. Both men were dark, gorgeous, and sexy. They exuded masculinity and had an innate presence that demanded attention. Dane had a cool elegance to his polished veneer and charm while Elliott was rugged, bold, and bodacious. When they were with me together, they were supportive, caring, and protective. When we were intimate together, I couldn't get enough of the carnal way they commanded my body and the ease of our time together afterward. When I had doubts, Dane looked after me. Whenever Elliott was around, he showed me kindness, and at times, raw passion. They never gave me the feeling that they were uncomfortable or jealous sharing me in bed. They had me wanting to see and be with them both again. Could I? Maybe once all this was resolved.

The knocks came again, calling me away from my reminiscing. I climbed out of bed and put on my robe then padded out of the bedroom to the front door with my mask in hand. When I went to reach for the doorknob, I hesitated.

Who would need to come to the suite right now?

I decided to ask through the door. "Who is it? Is there something wrong?"

There was silence at first, but then a deep male voice spoke from the other side. "Nothing to be alarmed about. We're doing checks." His tone was light, and under normal circumstances I'd have opened the door, but nothing about this trip was typical. With all the caution Dane and Elliott had taken by keeping me away from the rest of the people on board, it wouldn't be right to not be careful. Then again, as one of the 'kept' women, would it be expected of me to follow instructions? While I pondered, the doorbell rang again, followed by a rapid knock.

"I'll open the door, but could you please tell me who's doing the checks?" I asked. No answer came right away, and I thought perhaps the man left, but then came his answer: "Housekeeping."

The hairs on the back of my neck rose. Why would housekeeping need me to open the door? Wouldn't they have their own key if there was some sort of scheduled checks? Whatever was happening, I wasn't going to let this stranger in without Dane and Elliott being here.

"I'm sorry, but Dane—I mean, Mr. Westbrook and Mr. Carmichael are not in. They'll let you in when they return." My voice wavered slightly.

"Fine," said the man, and I let go of the breath I'd been holding in.

Jittery, I sat down on a couch to try to calm my nerves, which had jumped during the exchange. On the one hand, several staff members had come to deliver things during the time I'd been there, and all of them had asked before coming inside when they dropped off room service, or so I assumed. However, I couldn't remember if they entered with their own key or if Elliott or Dane answered for them. After a few minutes of debating, I concluded the man could as easily have a staff member give him a key should he need to return to the room to complete his checks. Hopefully, Dane or Elliott would return by then.

I tightened my robe. They both made me feel safe there. I waited a while then got up to see if they'd left a note.

What I discovered draped across one of the dinette chairs was the jeans and shirt I'd had on when I went to Dane's a few days before. Days—it seemed longer. I removed them from the hanger. If Dane had left them for me, it must've meant we were about to dock in San Francisco, which meant I would finally get to leave. Would Dane find Angel? Would they be safe?

My heart constricted. I wanted to leave, but I also wanted Dane and Elliott safe.

Returning to the bedroom, I decided to dress in my regular clothing. The bell sounded again while I was brushing my teeth, but I decided not to rush off to answer. The quiet when I turned off the water assured me they must have done whatever check they needed. Still, I put the mask back on, just in case they returned. I walked back into the bedroom, and then I stopped short.

A man was standing there in a leather jacket and black jeans with his back to me. He hadn't turned around, though my gasp was loud. Then he said, "About time you finished. You fucked up by making me go out and get someone to let me inside. I'll punish you for that. Kneel."

I didn't understand why he needed to be inside in the first place. Did Dane and Elliott know he was here?

My legs wobbled as I tried to assume the kneeling position Elliott had shown me, but not before I saw what he'd been doing. The man had a suitcase I recognized as Dane's out in front of him. The contents were scattered across the bedding.

My pulse sped up. "I was waiting for Dane and Elliott," I said in as calm a tone as I could manage. I wasn't sure if I should continue to speak, so I remained quiet and still on the floor while he continued his rifling. I froze. I was certain Dane wouldn't like him doing it, but I couldn't decide what to do. Then dark leather shoes entered my field of vision right before the pointed toe dug into my knee cap.

"Dane and Elliott? Not Mr. Westbrook and Mr. Carmichael?" he mocked, laughing at my mistake. "You don't address them as sir either. It's just like my uncle said: you all seem awfully familiar with each other and no one else here. I know everyone, and I don't know you. That's a problem we'll fix right now."

His hand suddenly closed on my head and tugged at my mask.

I gripped it and reared back as it came apart in his hands. My eyes inadvertently lifted to his face, and my mouth fell open. He still looked confused, like he didn't recognize me, but now that I could see his face fully, I instantly recognized him. It was Marco, Liz's boyfriend.

I went to lower my head again, but he grabbed my braid and yanked my head up toward him.

"You know me? Tell me how and I won't hurt you."

I wasn't fool enough to believe him, nor was I willing to keep the charade up to remain alone with him. Dane and Elliott hadn't ever left

335

me alone for long. They had to be on their way back now. I thought about the knife that was still in my robe, but if he was already trying to hurt me, what would he do if I used a weapon? I decided to remain calm. "I thought I knew you, but I don't. I'll wait for Mr. Westbrook and Mr. Carmichael to return."

"No, you won't." He yanked hard on my hair again and I stifled a whimper. "You're lying. Tell me the truth now, cunt."

He didn't wait for an answer, but drew his hand back to hit me.

Protocol be damned—I wasn't going to sit there and take a beating.

I punched his cock as hard as I could. He doubled over, but I didn't wait to see if it was enough to keep him down. As quickly as I could, I pushed to my feet and rushed out of the suite. The direness of the situation pressed down on me with every footfall.

I was in the hallway running down the deck in clothing but no mask—so much for not standing out again. Surprisingly, the deck was clear, and I stopped behind a door to try to figure out what to do. My eyes widened at what I saw in the sunrise: land. We had docked.

Were Elliott and Dane getting things in order so I could safely leave?

With Marco after me, I couldn't wait around any longer.

Turning a corner, I could see the exit sign ahead. If I could get off, I could tell someone to help me. I saw the sign for the stairs, but then I tumbled down and slammed hard on the deck, the wind completely knocked out of me.

Marco. He jumped up and yanked me to my feet by my arms then twisted them up my back as I cried out in pain.

"What's going on?" a man's voice yelled out. Marco didn't let me go when the guard came fully into view. His eyes shifted between us then settled on Marco. "Who is she?"

My breath staggered. "I'm with Mr. Westbrook and Mr. Carmichael. He came into their room and I caught him going through their things. He hurt me."

Marco twisted my arms harder and I yelped. "Shut up. She's hysterical."

"I should probably call this in." The guard took out his radio.

Marco guffawed. "You're taking the word of a lying bitch over me?" He scoffed. "She hit me." He let go of my arm then slapped me across my face, and I shrieked as stars filled my vision.

"Shit, man, you can't hit them before the trade show. Vincent will be upset," the guard said.

"Her face isn't what they want her for anyway," Marco replied with a snicker. "Vincent is my uncle and he runs this show, and you and no one else will do a damn thing about it. I don't know who she is, and she won't tell me, which is a problem. Just put this cunt in the limo. Send someone to clean their room so I can find out who she is."

"If she's with them, won't they be looking for her?" the guard asked as he took control of my arms, which were now sore.

"Dane disappointed my uncle, so he's uninvited to the trade show," he said dismissively. "If he comes looking, tell them she left."

"What about Elliott?" he asked. "He'll want details."

"Just give him a pick of the women," Marco told him. "He'll drop it. Hell, my uncle said he was trying to get rid of her last night, but Dane was acting like an asshole. We already have a plan for them anyway if they fuss too much."

Marco left me with the guard, and I struggled in his arms. Something sharp bit into my skin and I swayed.

"Now that should keep you quiet," the guard said as he slung me over his shoulder. I could just make out drops of my blood on the deck as we moved away from the stairs then onto the boarding ramp before everything went dark.

CHAPTER FIFTEEN

Hands shook my body. "You need to wake up."

The voice sounded like someone was calling me from the other end of a tunnel. I drew air into my lungs and was hit by pain in my chest and ribs. My cheek hurt, and so did my arms. The memory of how I'd gotten hurt was fuzzy at first, but with every painful breath I took, it became clearer. I had been attacked by Liz's boyfriend, Marco. He'd been upset that I recognized him and witnessed him going through Dane's things. His violence was chilling. Poor Liz. She'd been in pain the last time I saw her, when I didn't listen or insist on helping her.

Pain and remorse ate away at me. She could be hurt badly by now, or worse.

"Here's an ice pack. I'll be right back," said a female voice. Someone pressed cool gel on my face. The drug haze was losing its effect, and now, without effort, I opened my eyes and glanced around. The brightness of the light pouring in through the three large windows in the room took a few seconds to get used to. When my eyes adjusted, I could see a stunning panoramic view of the Golden Gate Bridge and blue skies. I was in San Francisco, but where?

I went to sit up on what I now saw was a four-poster bed and winced. My shirt and jeans were gone, leaving me in my underwear. Bruises stood out on my skin, but I was relieved that nothing had been broken. The band was still on my wrist. Dane and Elliott—they'd probably returned and realized I was gone. Were they looking? They must have thought I left.

If Marco and the guards searched the room, they must've found my identification by now, so they know I'm the ex of the governor of

Washington and a prominent business owner that was active in the community. They'll have to let me go.

That was what I kept telling myself as I took in my surroundings. The furnishings were a mixture of imported antiques, though more custom contemporary in styling. The bed I was on was near one of the two stone and marble fireplaces in the room. Each one had custom couches, tables, and lamps surrounding them, all perfectly set. The famous paintings and sculptures with authentications displayed throughout the room led me to believe this place didn't belong to someone who was just rich, but someone of great wealth. The closing of a door in the far left corner had me turning my attention there. An older woman in an old-fashioned black and white bibbed maid's uniform wheeled in a portable wardrobe that was twice as big as her. Her gray hair was platted closed to her scalp, making me think of pictures from the 1930s.

"Like my hair? I'll give yours some style too." She sat on the bed. "Maybe cover the side of your face to hide the bruise. Honestly, you're a bit of a mess. I don't know what you did, but try not to do it again or you'll attract the wrong man at the trade show."

"I don't understand," I asked. "What's a trade show?"

"You don't even know?" she said, flabbergasted. Then she shook her head. "Of course you don't. What were you promised? Cinderella stories?" She snickered. "You will find out there are no shortcuts in life. Everyone is paying, even those glamorous socialites you worship."

I opened my mouth and closed it. At one time, I had been one of those socialites she criticized, and in a way, she was right. I'd paid, and I'd built a new life, one I wanted to return to.

"All I know is that I was supposed to leave," I said after she helped to prop a pillow at my back. "I mean, I went to an Agency mixer and cruise..."

She patted my leg. "Don't worry, I know everything. Maybe it'll all come back to you once the sedative wears off."

"It's not the drug. I never got an answer on the trade show," I replied before clearing my throat.

"You were with a man who was taking care of you," she said. "But if you've been put in the pool of women they decided it didn't work out with them for whatever reason then you've been sent to the trade show. You'll still get your sweet deal, but with another sponsor of sorts." She spoke with unconcealed repulsion.

"I never asked for a *sweet deal* or a *sponsor*," I groused in frustration. "I'm not supposed to be here. I only went to one mixer—I'm not really a part of it. I had problems with my business and came to work on it with one of the people involved, but then I was forced into coming along. I don't belong here. I need to get home. Will you please help me? Do you know Dane Westbrook and Elliott Carmichael—"

She held up her hand for me to stop. Her eyes shifted from side to side, and I had to strain my ears to hear her. "Stop speaking. I have no power to help you here, at least not in the way you want." She pointed to the door and she didn't have to speak for me to understand that guards were outside.

I mouthed, "Send a message?"

She did a slow shake of her head and I deflated.

"I've never heard of those men you mentioned, and you haven't either," she cautioned before sighing heavily. "Now, let me help you in a way I can." She went over to the wardrobe and pulled out a high-collared, long-sleeved evening gown. The front was all lace and the flowing silk of the bottom half was long enough to cover my feet. "This will cover any bruises from what happened to your arm. The sheer material on your breasts will be attractive."

"I don't want to attract any of them," I grumbled.

"I understand, but Mr. Santiago is picking you up in the next hour. You must be ready." She pulled out a thong and silk stockings for me to wear with the heels that were set out. "You need to get dressed. It's the only way out without getting hurt. Choose your battles."

She helped me stand up, but I was conscious and coherent now. I went to change into the lace lingerie and the gown. She entered the bathroom and turned on the faucet.

"I have some e-comply," she whispered, showing me a tablet in her hand. "It'll help you to not remember all that they do to you."

They? My insides crumbled, but I refused, comforting myself by thinking I'd find a way out without her help by getting the information she would share. "What do they do?"

"Mostly sex, maybe try out some toys, spanks, clamps, whips," she said. "Some even more, but we'll try to get you to someone kind."

I doubted she'd have any control over who I went to. Besides, her speech seemed practiced, something she probably told many before me to get them to behave, but I wouldn't, nor would I get past the idea of pain.

"Are some of the men...sadists?" I asked.

"You wish," she said sadly. "Sadists play with those that are masochists. They play by rules and have limits. Most want to keep playing, not damaging their submissive beyond repair. These men have too much money and power to play around with. They like to raise the stakes for their own enjoyment."

I gasped and clutched my stomach. I wasn't leaving with any of them. *I will get out*, I kept repeating in my head.

"Keep your head down and don't cry. Tear streaks are an aphrodisiac for some here. Defiance is a challenge that some will work to break." She stared down at her hands. "The more you comply, the more freedom you'll get and the more options you'll have. The easier some of them have it, the less they will want to keep you."

"Why are you telling me this?" I whispered, fumbling as I struggled to put the silk stockings in place.

She met my eyes. "I'm not telling you anything, understand?"

I clasped her hand. "Thank you...?"

She shook her head. "No names."

She had said all she had for me. The second she was done styling my hair, the door opened to reveal the man I remembered was the guard who took me off the ship. My skin crawled as his gaze shifted up and down my body. I looked around for a mask, but there wasn't one. My identity would be revealed. Once it was, with all I'd witnessed, I doubted I'd be let go.

The guard let out a whistle. I grimaced, and the woman cleared her throat, reminding me what she had warned me about. I allowed him to take my arm. *For now, until I find my escape.*

"You're beautiful, baby girl," he said. "Maybe the host will let the guards play with you before he has to turn you over."

"She's for the host?" the woman asked, the alarm in her voice evident.

The only host I knew was Vincent, but that didn't surprise me. It had become personal between him and Dane during the evening we were together. What was making my pulse ramp up to a frantic pace was the news that I was to be turned over to someone else. They hadn't removed my wristband. Could it be that they would give me back to Dane? The question was out of my mouth before I could stop it.

"Turn me over to who?" I demanded.

The guard looked straight through me. "Whoever they please." He took my arm and my hope.

***

Outside the room was an elevator that took us down to a private underground garage where a limousine was waiting. The guard let go of my arm and opened the back door, where Marco appeared and climbed out.

"Gia Walsh," Marco said, grinning. He used my married name—did he not know I was divorced? I didn't seek to correct him, but it gave me an idea.

I shrugged. "If you know my name, you also know I'm the wife of Washington's governor, Patrick Walsh Jr. You need to let me go now."

He chuckled. "That's the very reason you can't go, stupid," he said in a mocking tone. "But don't you worry, once you adjust to your new life, you'll be fine, just like your friend Liz. She said she knows you, told me everything about you."

I swallowed. Of course Liz had to tell him about me if she found out I was here. I only hoped he hadn't hurt her to get the information. "Liz is here?"

"Yes, she is," he said, like he'd given me a gift. He gestured toward the open door of the limo. "She can't wait to speak to you."

I held my tongue and didn't move away when he stroked my cheek.

"See? I'm good when you behave," he purred, taking my silence as compliance.

I needed to stay focused until I could escape.

"You and Liz stay good and we can all have fun together." He pressed his hand on my back and I climbed inside the vehicle then watched him go back inside the house just as the driver moved the limo.

"Gia!" Liz exclaimed as the door closed. The sight of her left me temporarily speechless.

Liz was sitting across from me. She was...radiant. She was well dressed in a strapless satin evening gown a shade darker than her red hair, which swept to the side in stylish waves. The shawl I'd loaned her was folded neatly next to her on a plush leather seat.

"Thank God you've woken up," she said. Her eyes shone. "I was shocked when they brought you inside Marco's house. I begged them to get a doctor, but—"

My jaw tightened. "You knew about them taking me?"

She shook her head. "No. I didn't know you were here. I was at the house of one of Marco's friends overnight. I only arrived back at his place this morning. He and I aren't together anymore." She stifled a sob. "It's all complicated...I tried to warn you to stay away from The Agency members, but here you are."

Seeing that she was distressed, I decided not to point out how vague she'd been at the time, but I couldn't blame it all on her. No one knows when or where danger comes. We learn after it's done.

"Did Marco hit you too?" I asked. "That time at the gym."

"No, that wasn't him," she said. "He didn't like that I was jealous of him being with someone else. He offered to 'make it up to me' by giving me to his uncle for the night. He went from treating me so kindly to treating me like trash... I'm devastated that he hurt you."

My hand clasped Liz's. I didn't blame her. I was grateful she had tried to help me, though the thought of hours lost from my life was disturbing. It couldn't have been easy when they found out she knew me. The lump lodged in my throat made it hard to swallow. "He made you talk about me."

She blinked back tears, reached into a small clutch for a handkerchief, and dabbed her eyes. "Yes. I was upset when I saw you and was told I had to tell them everything I knew about you. I told them you were a governor's wife, but I don't think that helped."

I would have thought it'd give me leverage, but not with these men.

"They plan to take you to the trade show, do you know that?" she asked in a hushed tone.

"Yes," I said as I coughed.

She reached over, took out a bottled water from a hidden drawer, and handed it to me. I drank down almost all of it.

"How did you find out about it?" she asked.

"Dane and Elliott," I said, and a pang went through my chest. They were being told I had left. Would they believe it or do anything rash?

She sighed heavily. "I thought so, but from what I understand, this will not turn out as bad. There will be something like that orgy, but then you will be chosen by a man who will keep you. You'll discuss what they could do for you and what they expect. In the end, everything will work out. You'll be better off financially."

I scoffed. "What money do either one of us need?"

"Come on, Gia. Everyone knows you've lost your company," she said. "My own money has been frozen for an investigation into my late husband's assets."

I started to say that was impossible, but then it all started to make sense. Angel, Liz, me—I now completely understood The Agency. The powerful men created situations for women who were strong and successful, women who didn't need them, so they could play with or break them for their own amusement...but could there be more to their choices? While I worked it over in my mind, trying to figure it all out, Liz lamented.

"This is all my fault." Liz sniffed. "The Agency, the men were too good to be true...and I found out they were. They know everyone we know, so there is no escape. I was told if I cooperate, everything will return to normal or better. He said I'd be able to get my business back on track."

I closed my eyes. That was what Dane's Angel must have thought. They didn't return her to her life, and from what Marco said, I knew too much to leave. Dread swallowed me whole. I didn't see a return. We both needed to get out of there.

"Listen to me, Dane and Elliott would help us—"

"Save your breath. They knew I was here with Marco," Liz said, cutting me off. "They are Agency men. Where were they when you were taken?"

My throat closed. I didn't have the answers, but I couldn't believe Dane or Elliott would do this to me. She had to be wrong.

"You cause no trouble and you return to Seattle," she said. "You obey, and things could get even better for you. The man I met that Marco's trading me to is getting me a new penthouse in Seattle and a vacation house in Spain. He has a lawyer already working on my financial problems."

The financial problems he and his friends created for you for their own sick entertainment. I scowled. I couldn't believe Liz was getting caught up in their lies. "You tell me not to trust, but you trust they'll hold up their end of the bargain with you?"

"We'll just have to see," she said, leaving out the fact that we had no other choice.

I pursed my lips. "But they are so transparent, and you really believe a man who's making us go is actually going to help you?"

She didn't respond, and we stopped speaking. Liz was in survival mode. I was too, but my plan was not to cooperate. I was going to get away and call the number Dane had given me for his lawyer. The second I found a way to get a call or message out, I would say where I was and hopefully get the police to come rescue me. I wanted to believe my plan was possible, but then doubt crept in. What if Liz had been right all along? Why was I willing to just think the other men were bad and not Dane and Elliott? Dane was about to do all the things Liz was claiming this new man was going to do for her. Had I been equally naïve?

The car moved onto the highway. I decided to keep a mental note of markers. AT&T park, the Embarcadero...we were going toward the pier. With all the pedestrian traffic, I was sure it would be easier to get out and escape. My hopes diminished when we exited and turned under a bypass. This wasn't one of the bustling picturesque areas of the city; it was a construction site with boarded fences and scaffolding. No one would go there unless they were working on the building. An Agency member probably owned the site, so no one there would help us.

The limo turned down a dead-end road and drove underneath a scaffold-fronted building to an underground parking garage then out the other side to a driveway. At the end was a row of three brand new Victorian-style homes in various stages of completion. We parked at the most finished one, and an armed guard opened the door. He was surprisingly gentle when he helped us out of the car, though he stayed close behind us the rest of the way up the driveway.

Once inside, we were taken into a formal dining room with fabric and mahogany paneling and a grand chandelier as its centerpiece. Besides the beautiful handmade ornamental rugs, four floral-patterned pastel lounge chairs were the only seating in the room and were set up near one of the two fireplaces. Two of the chairs were already occupied by women dressed as formally as Liz and I were. It was quite the contrast from the boat. They were also unmasked, but I didn't recognize them.

The guard motioned for Liz and me to take the open seats, and we sat down on one next to each other.

I was relieved to see him turn to go, but then high-pitched laughter filled the room. I looked over to find a wraithlike woman with eyes that were too big for her face sauntering over to us. Her blonde hair was curly and swept up in a chignon. She had on a silk evening gown made of shimmering fabric, and golden rings looped through her pale skin ran the length of her back. I stared at them when she spun around before us.

"If you're scared of this, let me assure you, it will get worse," she sang out at the end of the room.

"Now Angel, behave," one of the guards said to her. He came forward and tried to take her arm.

Angel jerked away from him, and he let her. "No. I'm in the trade show today and I get to stay."

"Not if you cause trouble," he whispered.

"You don't control me," she hissed at him then started laughing again. He followed her around the room as she continued her spectacle, trying to stop her from knocking over vases and lamps, tilting pictures on the walls, or picking up the pillows on the back of the lounge chairs to throw on the floor. One of the women tried to help him keep the order, and that I didn't understand. The rest of us stared at Angel in shock. I couldn't believe this was the same woman who'd headed her own company. I elbowed Liz and gave her a hard look. Liz didn't know Angel, but she had to see that the woman before us was where we were all headed if we didn't do something about it.

Liz cast her eyes down, and I sighed in acceptance. Whatever I chose to do, I'd be doing it without her help.

"Mommy, Mommy." A little girl toddled into the room in a pink party dress with little wings. She had springy blonde curls, the same color as Angel's. She brushed her chubby little hand on our dresses as she passed by. "Pretty...pretty...pretty..."

Could she be Dane's? When she approached my seat, I quickly put my hands on my knees. Her hand tapped my own and she paused. Her eyes—which were so like his—met my own, and my heart broke. I'd seen her before he had the chance. I didn't think for a minute Dane would give up his daughter. Her being there proved Liz was wrong about him and Elliott.

"Angel, Melinda's here," the guard said, taking the little girl's hand.

Angel didn't turn around. She stared out the window.

"Get her out of here." Vincent's voice came from the archway. "Where is the nanny they brought with them?"

I recognized the woman in uniform from Marco's home as she came rushing in and swept the child up in her arms. The guard followed her out before pulling a pocket door to close off the room.

"I see you're all here," Vincent said, walking over to the fireplace. He was dressed in a shirt and trousers, almost casual. Above where he stood was a painting of a younger man who resembled him. Marco had been right about taking us to his uncle's home. "You four had to come here first because we think you need more training. Angel, come over and show the girls how to get into position."

Angel quickly rushed over to him and dropped to her knees.

He petted her head. "How about you show the others how we want them to behave at the show?"

She lay down on her back and pulled up her dress then slid down her panties. She bowed her legs out, revealing her bare sex before him.

"Now spread your lips," he demanded.

My stomach lurched, and I turned my head away from the display. *I'd never do that*, I thought, yet a seed of doubt planted in my head. What if the man that bought me drugged and hurt me?

"You're perfect baby girl," he cooed to her. "That's good training. You will all learn to be just as willing to please when asked. It will be like one long green mixer at the trade shows, but the rest of the time will be mostly yours, as long as you behave. You have access to the best men in the world, and once things are settled, you won't want to leave."

It was a struggle to school my face. I didn't care who they were; I'd go to the police the second I was free. It was as if Vincent plucked the plan from my mind.

"Leaving won't help your situation," he said. "It'll get worse. Who but us could right your accounts, get judges to throw out any ruling against you in court? Without one of our backings, you could end up humiliated, ruined, and in jail. You'll lose it, trust me."

I bristled. *Like I'd ever trust you.*

The door pushed back and a guard stuck his head inside. "The men are all here."

"Great," he said. "Now Angel, I need you to wait upstairs."

She sat up on her knees and started rocking. "I've been good."

"Yes, but these ladies haven't worked out, so I've got to work with them before they go to the show," he explained in a childlike voice. He pulled the silk at her back, causing her skin to stretch into little peaks, and she moaned. "Don't worry, I'll give you a playmate to take back with you once we're done."

Her eyes widened. "He said to pack everything. I'm going back?"

He snickered. "Of course you are baby girl. You wouldn't want to leave your home. You've got mansions, cars, servants, and your daughter. Why would you want to leave?"

Angel leaned toward his ear like she was going to whisper a secret. He blew out his breath and cocked his ear. She came close to him and laughed loudly.

"Stop," Vincent said, yanking harder on the fabric at her back, but Angel didn't comply. She laughed louder and louder until the room was filled with her high-pitched shrieks.

Vincent glowered at her and yelled, "Get her out of here now." He tried to push her forward, but she didn't fall. The guard came in, swept her off her feet, and carried her out.

I snickered. If only she could have ruptured his eardrum.

He came over to stand in front of me. "You find that amusing? No wonder one of your lovers called me this morning to bring you here."

I pressed my lips together. "You're lying."

"Oh good." He chuckled. "I was hoping to be the one to break this news to you." He next called the guard over. Liz was escorted out with the other women, leaving me alone with him, but not for long. My heart dropped to my feet. Coming through the door in a suit and tie was none other than Elliott Carmichael, the very man I thought was Dane's best friend and my ally. He strolled over to Vincent and they gave each other a hug. Hatred took hold of me. I'd been completely blindsided. I hadn't fully understood Elliott, but I couldn't believe he'd betrayed me. I bit the inside of my cheek hard to stop myself from falling apart, but I was losing the battle. *Is Dane here too?*

"Miss me, baby?" Elliott said to me as he winked.

"Fuck off," I hissed, and Vincent laughed.

"You were right." Vincent chuckled. "Seeing her face when you came in was worth having you here."

"You should have let me take her off the ship." He glanced over my face. "It would have gone better than using Marco."

Vincent cursed. "Yeah. Marco is as much a disappointment as Dane. You smoothed that over?"

"Yes, I did," Elliott said. He took out a key I recognized as the one Dane had used to lock the band on my wrist. "He thinks she left with me and by the time he finds out, he'll just think she wanted to put it all behind her and stay away from him."

"You fucking asshole," I shrieked. "How could you do that to him after all you know—"

"Shut the hell up," Elliott said through gritted teeth. He came over and clasped the sides of my face. His eyes bore into mine. "Or will we need to drug you again?" His voice dropped to a whisper. "Like I told you before:

367

you try to escape, and I'll turn everything upside down to find you."

I blinked at him in confusion. What he said was close to what he'd told me before.

Did that mean he was there to help me, or was this more betrayal? I wouldn't risk it.

I jerked away, and his head nodded before he swung back around to Vincent. "See? A pain in the ass. That's why I want rid of her. Dane seemed to like the challenge."

Vincent shrugged. "I'm with Dane—I like them feisty. You should see the one that came over from our European chapter. She was a spitfire when I saw her once before, a few years ago, but now she's kind of slow."

I swallowed. Angel.

"If she's that messed up, why not cut her loose?" Elliott asked. The sound of sirens temporarily made it hard to hear Vincent's answers. My heart beat harder when they came close, but then the sound faded again.

"I got a call to pick her up for the trade today," he said as he sat down on a lounge chair next to me. "The man that had Angel kept her too long and was stupid. It happens sometimes. He's in the hospital over here, getting surgery for something rare. We are planning to kick him out. So, we hope to find one of you to take her. He had picked out Dane, and even wanted us to do a video stream so he could see her going to him, but Dane brought Gia and was an ass about hiding her, so he's out. I head up the trade shows. I decide who gets to play."

I sneered at him. Vincent was full of shit as much as he was of information. He wouldn't say his name, but what the man who'd kept Angel had against Dane was apparently personal. The Agency wasn't just about taking women; it was also about revenge. The absolute cruelty of the man who'd kept Angel for years made me cringe. He must have known all along who she was, and Dane, possibly the real Dane...Dane Prescott. It made me sick to think he wanted to watch Dane be destroyed by seeing what he and his buddies had reduced Angel to.

If that weren't horrible enough, he'd also meet the child he never knew.

"Sounds like a good plan," Elliott said, and they laughed together. "But you shouldn't talk in front of her."

Vincent shrugged. "Why not? She can't go home. I might as well keep her...it's a shame Angel's keeper is sick," Vincent said then turned to me. "He does good training. When he recovers, I might let him have Gia for a week before we kick him out."

His calloused fingers stroked my cheek and I swiped his hand away.

He scoffed. "I'm too old for brats. When you start behaving like an *angel*, you will have more freedom. Could someone get her some e-comply?"

Whatever these men did had made Angel go insane. I wasn't taking any more drugs or giving in.

I stood up, and Elliott grabbed my sore arms. "Sit down."

I jerked out of his hold. "I'm not going to sit here and let him drug and rape me. I don't care about money, lifestyle, or any of this shit. Just take it all and let me go."

"Whatever you want to do, Vince," Elliott offered, ignoring me.

Vincent held up his hand. "Someone get in here now." He called out for a guard again, but no one came. I looked around for a way out as minutes passed.

Elliott grumbled as I twisted in his hold again. "What's taking so long?"

"I'll be back." Vincent pushed the door wider and walked through the gap, yelling, "Didn't you hear me calling for you?"

I took a step away from Elliott, and he took my arm back.

"Do you know it's Angel upstairs? She's lost her mind and she has Dane's little girl. She's here in this horrible place. How could you?" I choked.

He put his hand over my mouth. "Shut up or I'll gag you." He removed his hand but quickly took hold of my arms.

I stomped the heel of my stiletto into the top of his shoe. "I hate you. You will all rot in hell for this."

He didn't even flinch. "Good, you've stopped trying to find my good side."

"You don't have one," Marco said, and then he laughed as he came through the door holding up a syringe. "Uncle Vincent had to go check on something. We can start the party first."

Elliott let go of my arms and placed his hands on my shoulders, moving me flush against his body.

"Let her go," Marco commanded. "I want her to fight me again."

I sneered. *Oh, please let him, Elliott. I've got fight for him.*

Elliott smiled at me. "You heard him. He wants a fight."

I didn't hesitate. I jumped onto Marco and we fell to the floor together, hard. He shifted around to try to find the syringe he'd dropped, but I was back on him, hitting, scratching, ripping at his clothing. I was doing anything I could to stop him from getting a hold of the drug again.

"You fucking bitch." He hissed and pushed me hard in the chest, knocking me off him.

I fell back in pain and gasped for breath.

"What the hell?" A guard came in and Elliott rushed over and knocked him over on his side. I pulled at the fabric of the dress to free it from under Marco, who was fighting to get a hold of me. He tugged hard against my grasp, tearing the material covering my waist.

I kicked out with my legs, but the long dress made it hard to connect with his body. He didn't have the same problem. His leg kicked out and landed on my sore ribs, and I screamed in agony.

"You will pay for this, bitch," Marco hissed.

I smirked. Guess he hadn't expected a real fight.

Marco was quick to straddle my body and pin me down. "Don't bother looking for Elliott. He won't be around to help you any time soon," he said roughly.

I reached between his legs and grabbed hold of his balls then squeezed with all I had.

Marco yelled out, "You're dead!" Then he grabbed my neck and squeezed.

I clawed with my fingers and twisted my body under him.

Elliott came into my line of sight behind him. He had the syringe in his hand.

"Elliott, get out of here now. You know you're done," Marco told him as he struggled to keep a hold of me. "You interfere, and we'll kill you both."

Elliott plunged the syringe into Marco's arm. "Vincent won't be coming back. This is an FBI raid, motherfucker."

Marco's eyes bulged, and he tried to hit at Elliott but was too slow.

Elliott stood and kicked him over to his side. I scooted across the carpet away from him, my breath labored as I tried to understand what Elliott had said to him. "You're...FBI?"

Elliott smiled. "I'll explain later."

He kicked Marco in the ribs. "That's for hurting Gia, though it still isn't enough." I gaped at him as he patted Marco down until he found a gun strapped to his lower leg. He removed it from the holster and armed it.

My mouth dropped open. I hadn't even considered that he could be armed. "He could have killed me."

"This is not the time," he said. "I need to go see what's going on."

My eyes darted from Marco to the doorway. "Don't leave me in here," I stammered.

He cupped my face. "Marco will be out for hours. I'll push the guard out and block the doors. I promise I won't let anything happen to you. We will leave here together."

"Yes. You both will be leaving." Vincent appeared at the door with a police officer behind him. "You're under arrest."

CHAPTER SIXTEEN

"Put the gun down," the officer yelled out. "A man is down, get an ambulance," he shouted into his radio

"It's like I told you," Vincent said, "this was a private party, and they brought drugs in. That's my nephew on the ground. You get them out of here now, or my next call will be to your superior."

"Move away from me Gia," Elliott told me. He next turned to the police officer. "You're going to take out the gun and point it at me and I'm going to remove my badge from my jacket pocket."

The officer took out his gun.

"No," I said frantically. "I won't move away. Look at my torn dress. He and his nephew brought me here against my will. This man rescued me."

"She's lying, and he has a gun," Vincent pointed out. "Shoot him."

"You must, Gia," Elliott said. "Do it now, slowly."

I moved to the side, and the officer raised the gun at Elliott, who raised his hands.

Another officer entered the room and announced, "Ambulance is on its way."

"No ambulances," Vincent said. "I just want them and all of you out of my home— now." His voice reverberated off the walls.

"Sorry Mr. Santiago," the first police officer said. "He identified himself as FBI. We have to check it out." He turned to the other officer. "Go frisk him."

The officer took Elliott's gun then patted him down. "He's wired."

"We got you recorded, asshole," Elliott said. "My team should be nearby or already outside the gate. I'll give you the number to the head of the operation."

"That has to be illegal," Vincent flustered.

The officer continued to search Elliott. He pulled his wallet from his front left pocket and flipped through it.

"He's telling the truth," the officer said then handed Elliott his badge.

"I don't care," Vincent said to the officer. "He and his women came here under false pretenses. This was a private party on my property."

Elliott moved over to stand in front of me. "I'll go when I see you in handcuffs. He kidnapped Gia Walsh."

"I'm a well-respected member of this community," Vincent asserted. "Who is she?"

"I'm Gia...Walsh. Governor Walsh's wife, from Seattle," I said. "I was drugged and abused by this man and his nephew."

"I never abused you," Vincent fumed.

The police officer went over to Vincent. "Mr. Santiago, you'll have to come down to the station with us."

"I'm calling my lawyers," Vincent said then stormed out of the room.

Elliott placed his arm around me. "You okay, baby?"

I bristled. "Don't call me baby."

"Sweetheart, I told you I'd turn everything upside down to find you."

Our eyes lingered and mine filled. He had. He'd saved me. Tears streamed down my face and he gently placed his arm around my shoulder.

I winced in pain but didn't move out of his embrace.

Elliott took off his jacket and helped me put it on to cover myself, and I appreciated it. "We need an EMT. To take...Ms. Walsh to the hospital."

He led me and the others out to the hallway, back toward the grand stairway where Vincent was standing, talking on his phone. I didn't see any of the men and women who had been there. Had they let them all leave?

"We wiretapped your calls too, but you can keep talking," Elliott told Vincent.

"You'll end up the one in trouble," Vincent said as he scowled.

A high-pitched laugh rang out from the top of the stairs. *Angel.*

We all turned as she descended with a gun in her hand.

"She's sick," I cried out. "Angel, put the gun down. It's over. We can all leave."

"Drop the weapon," one of the officers said, pulling his gun out.

She didn't. She pointed it at Vincent and fired. Elliott pushed me back. "Get on the ground. Angel!" His cry was loud, but there was nothing we could do to stop what had happened.

Red exploded on the front of her body and she fell, rolling the rest of the way down, her body landing in a twisted heap at the bottom.

Elliott rushed over and pulled her on her back. "Shit. Get me something to help her—towels, something."

The housekeeper came running over to hand Elliot a cloth and he pressed it to the wound. "Angel, come on, don't give up now." His voice shook.

All I could think of was Dane. He'd been so close to getting Angel back, only to have her taken without her knowing that he tried to save her.

The other officer joined him. I looked around and found Vincent far down the hall, away from us. He appeared unharmed, but there was an officer standing guard over him, making sure he didn't try to leave.

The front door opened and officers and EMTs entered. They took over and loaded Angel on the gurney.

"Mommy, Mommy!" Melinda came running out of one of the closed rooms with the maid close behind her. My heart shattered as she tried to get close to her mother.

"Get her out of here," Elliott barked, using his body to block the little girl from seeing.

I scrambled to my feet and swept her into my arms. "It's going to be okay."

"Mommy okay?" she asked.

They moved her out the door.

"I'll take her," Vincent said. "Come on Melinda."

"Is she your child, Mr. Santiago?" asked the police officer standing next to him.

"I...I...her mother had stopped by," he stuttered. "I can see that she goes to her father."

I seethed. Was he angling for some sort of leverage to avoid going to jail or to keep Angel silent by trying to take her child? There was no way he was getting anywhere near their child.

"Back the fuck up," I said through clenched teeth. "Her father, Dane, should be close by. He will take her."

Vincent blinked. *Now who's surprised?* The Agency must not have told him.

Apparently, he wasn't as high up in their membership as he thought.

"She's right," Elliott said. "I'll get him to meet us at the hospital."

"Where is everyone?" I asked as Elliott guided Melinda and me out the front door and over to an ambulance.

"I don't know." He took out his phone, and Melinda stared at me quizzically.

"That's your...your Uncle Elliott. He will get you to your mommy," I said gently.

He pinched his eyes before taking her in his arms. He waited until the emergency staff checked me out and placed me on a gurney for transport.

"Come here for a second." He called over an officer to hold Melinda then climbed in the back of the ambulance with me. That was when I let go of everything I had bottled up since I'd been taken.

I let out a sob. "Thank you."

He took my lips and pressed down on them hard. "I've got some things to do here, but I won't be long."

"I just want to go home," I murmured.

He stroked my face. "You're getting checked out at the hospital. They'll need a statement too."

I grinned. Elliott Carmichael, FBI— shocking.

"Sure, officer," I tried to joke.

"Soon to be ex-FBI," he said. "I enjoyed being an interior designer."

Was he teasing? It didn't matter right then. He'd been there when I needed him. He'd saved me, Angel, and Melinda. He'd helped Dane. "Thank you."

He pressed his lips to my forehead. "You didn't need much help, you ball-busting badass. I'm blown away by you."

I giggled then winced in pain. I owed him my life.

The emergency workers moved him out and hooked up an IV then I was off to the hospital. I closed my eyes, my head spinning with everything that had happened. It was so sensational that I doubted anyone would believe me, but with the recordings, there was proof.

Once there, I was faced with an explosion of media cameras flashing as I exited from the back of the ambulance. News traveled fast. Then again, a sitting governor's ex-wife getting kidnapped was too sensational of a story to pass up. I was sure to be hearing from Patrick. For once, I didn't care.

After they bandaged my bruises and treated my face, I was left alone in a hospital room to rest. When I opened my eyes again, the room was full of roses, and Dane. He was sitting in a chair close to my bed. It was a version of Dane I hadn't seen before. His shirt was creased, dark hair tousled, a day's growth of beard on his face. In other words, he looked amazing.

"You're awake," he said as he touched my cheek lightly. "You were hurt. I'm sorry I wasn't there. Vincent called me to meet him and then I was immediately ejected from the boat. I had to depend on Elliott to see you through, and then Angel, and...Melinda."

The pain on his face made my heart turn over. I reached out and took his hand. "I'm sorry, Dane. We tried for Angel, but...how is she now? How is Melinda?"

Dane's eyes shimmered. "Angel is in intensive care, and Melinda is here in a family room with a nurse. I caused all your suffering." His voice cracked.

"Stop that," I said. "You never gave up. We are safe because of you and Elliott. I'm thankful." More than thankful—they'd saved my life.

"Still, I should have been there." He picked up an envelope and handed it to me. "I couldn't be there like I wanted to, but I did take the time to get this for you."

It was a receipt for money to keep my company afloat, and a first-class ticket back to Seattle.

A flutter went through my chest. Dane had kept his promise. "Thank you."

A knock sounded on the door. "You busy?" Elliott asked. He came over and put his hand on Dane's shoulder. "Melinda is with the nurse."

I swallowed hard, but I understood. Angel and Melinda needed him. "You should go."

Dane nodded then leaned over and kissed my lips tenderly. "I should stay too, but I won't be far."

"Gia's tough. She'll be all right," Elliott said with a wink at me.

Dane kissed me and whispered, "You never have to be tough with me."

"Or you with me," I whispered back.

A million things went through my head as I watched Dane leave the room. Dane's love and care were boundless. He'd turned his world upside down for Angel. To really know him and have his heart would be something to cherish.

I sighed. *They need him.*

"Whatever you're thinking now, Dane's not gone if you want him to stay," Elliott said to me.

"You think so?" I murmured.

"I do," Elliott answered. "He wouldn't leave you."

I bit my lip. "Will you Elliott? Now that you've finished with The Agency?" I couldn't ask if he was finished with me. I didn't know where I stood with him most of the time, but what I was sure of was that we shared something more than friendship.

"The Agency case isn't over and done yet," Elliott said as he took my hand. "I'm here now. How are you feeling? I hate that I couldn't stop him from hitting you, but I needed his confession—"

"You did the right thing. I'm fine," I said then cleared my throat. "Whatever can stop what happened from happening again is worth living through a few bruises. Where are the other women? Liz?"

"Vincent convinced the first officer on scene to let the women leave with the men," Elliott told me. "But with all we know now, they won't get far."

I appreciated his optimism. Then again, most of the men would probably want to distance themselves from this scandal once it became public.

Elliott took the envelope Dane had given me from my shaky hands. "We'll fly back to Seattle together as soon as the doc says you're free to go."

I was free to return to the life I'd known, but now I was more than miles away from cosmetic samples and Christmas-tinis.

THANK YOU READERS!

If you enjoyed the INDISCREET: The Agency Dark Affairs Duet Book One. I hope you had fun reading this story as much as I had writing it. Book Two DAUNTLESS will be available soon.

VISIT AMÉLIE S. DUNCAN'S OFFICIAL WEBSITE

at WWW.AMELIESDUNCAN.COM

SUBSCRIBE TO AMÉLIE S. DUNCAN'S MAILING LIST

Updates on new releases and giveaways only

SUBSCRIBE NOW

Follow me

INSTAGRAM: AMELIE S. DUNCAN'S INSTAGRAM

AMAZON: AMELIE S. DUNCAN

AMAZON FOLLOW PAGE

ACKNOWLEDGMENTS

Thank you, my dear husband and best friend Alan. Here we are again. I love you so much.

A wonderful group of people helped me with INDISCREET. I greatly appreciate all your hard work.

Thank you, Silvia Curry, Lisa M. Birch, Deanna, Amy, Cynthia and Persephone, for their beta critiques. Thank you all for your kindness, support, and patience.

Thank you, Caitlin at Editing by C. Marie, for copy editing.

Thank you, Kim Ginsberg, for proofreading.

Thank you Roxana Cousmans for final proofreading.

Thank you, Sommer Stein of Perfect Pear Creative, for cover design.

Thank you Michelle New for the teasers.

Thank you to my friends, bloggers and reviewers for all your kindness and support in the promotion.

Thank you, readers, for reading this story. I most sincerely hope you enjoyed it.

ABOUT THE AUTHOR

mélie S. Duncan writes Contemporary and Erotic Romances. Her inspiration comes from many sources including her life experiences and travels. She lives on the West Coast of the United States with her husband.

ALSO BY AMÉLIE S. DUNCAN

Match Fit (Love and Play Series) Book One

Match Made (Love and Play Series) Book Two

The Tiger Lily: An Alpha Billionaire Romance Trilogy

The Piper Dreams: A New Adult Romance Trilogy

Little Wolf: A Dark Erotic Standalone

Made in the USA
Las Vegas, NV
04 March 2023

68532569R00223